CW00550607

good deed rain

OUR STORY BEGINS with The House of Stars, a place for tourists who wandered off the boulevard, drawn to the seedier side of town. There was no air conditioning, it was a hundred degrees and then some. The wax museum was melting, and Voyd Lewismeter carried the Beatles outside in a wheelbarrow.

HOLOGRAMS from MARS

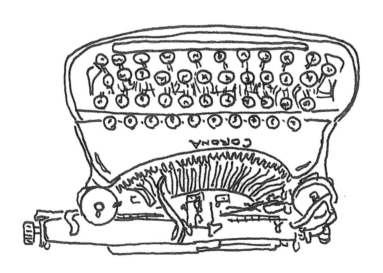

HOLOGRAMS from MARS © 2024
Allen Frost, Good Deed Rain
Bellingham, Washington
ISBN: 979-8-8690-8038-7

Writing and Drawings: Allen Frost
Cover Painting:
"Familiar Reflections" by Emma Toscani
Cover Production: Fred Sodt
Apple: TFK!

Credits:

Nathaniel Hawthorne, *The American Notebooks*, Ohio State University Press, 1932.

Ed Wood script for *The Ghoul Goes West*, 1951, from *Ed Wood and the Lost Lugosi Screenplays*, by Gary D. Rhodes, BearManor Media, 2016.

Norma Shearer in *Idiot's Delight*, MGM, 1939.

HOLOGRAMS from MARS

Allen Frost

Good Deed Rain ◊ Bellingham, Washington ◊ 2024

To write a dream, which shall resemble the real course of a dream, with all its inconsistency, its strange transformations, which are all taken as a matter of course, its eccentricities and aimlessness—with nevertheless a leading idea running through the whole. Up to this old age of the world, no such thing ever has been written.

—Nathaniel Hawthorne

I was exiled for my imagination. I came to this country then—to this little community, where I could continue my experiments in relative safety and secrecy.

—Edward D. Wood, Jr.

Maybe we're the only ones in this crazy world who are real.
—Norma Shearer

Slot machines.
A slot machine on the corner of the Boulevard.
Need to pay toll to cross street. Put coin
in slot and the dial spins. He watches arrow
stop on 10 minutes.
"I'll go to another corner. "
Person next to him rolls her eyes. "Let me try."

Voyd is robot repairman.

8/21/23

Lives next door to a cathedral
It was a cheap trick. A hologram was
transplanted over what their house really
looked like. There are other houses like
that too. He goes on call to fix a house
that's a Bait Shack. He supposes as he
gets closer ~~and~~ he will pass through the
hologram but it stays a bait shack. Problem
is with aquarium motor for the mermaid
tank. "They sent a guy to do a city-wide
test. " Voyd says, "I know him, He's my
nemesis. "

FOREWORD

Hi, I'm the author. I'm inviting you to an exclusive behind-the-scenes look at this new novel. I have 24 notebook pages written in preparation and I'm ready to start. The road lies ahead, there's a Martian on the boulevard. I have a pretty good idea what's going to happen next. For now, I'll follow my outline, but I expect that journey to change. Who knows? We'll find out as we go. Welcome to *Holograms from Mars!*

CHAPTERS

The House of Stars

Blunder

The Next Morning

A Familiar-Looking Man

The War Against the Wax Museum

Every Martian's Dream

The Wolf at the Zoo

Dinosaurs

The Fosbury Boy

A Paper Boat

Bonita

Job #17

Nirvana

Working

Wishbone

Marjorie Stars

Hidden Talents

The Charo Anecdote

Alphabet Trouble

On the Trolley

In a Blackberry River

The Martian Dollar

Wish List

The Gift of Life

Martian Intuition

Up and Over

Led to the Zoo

The Smoking Hand

Whistling

Sirens

Another Don

Flicker

The Martian Machinery

Extraordinary

Betty Grable

Their Window

The Martian Loyalty Oath

Sterling Hayden

Near Zephyria

The Al Pacino Postcard

Helping a Fellow Martian

Walking to Safeway

D's Memory

A Day's Travel

The New Atmosphere
Turning in Time
Better Vacuums
The Hoover Constellation
Tokyo Piano
Starlings
Torchy Blane
The Sound of the Rain
Other Messages
A Return Rocket at Dawn
The Multiple Dimensions of Reincarnation
The Song in the Air
The Sweeper
The Morning Herald
Martian Radio
Look Out Any Window
Pheasant Street
The Red Planet Wavelength
A Tin Peach Can
The Same Fish
Take Your Time
Rest

1
The HOUSE of STARS

It was a hot August afternoon on the boulevard and the wax museum was melting. Amelia Earhart floated in a pool on the floor and all her companions were going fast too. The air-conditioner had been dismantled since closing time yesterday and the owner arrived at work late to find radiators going full-steam instead. The museum was like an oven. He ran in and out of the back door, stacking the unfortunate stars in the alley shadows. They slumped against each other in unsplendor.

That was when Voyd stepped off the streetcar at his stop, lost in thought, turned the corner onto Crow Street and noticed The House of Stars. The front door was open, a crayon trickle seeped from it onto the sidewalk. Someone was shouting inside. It sounded like Peter Lorre meeting his end. Several people had stopped, some were helping, some were standing there unsure of what to do. Someone ran out the door with half of Una Merkel and took off down the street. Voyd left his thoughts and hurried across the road.

The owner, a thickset man named Bernard, stood in the doorway and shouted for help.

"What can I do?" Voyd asked when he got there.

"We have to get the figures outside! Quick, please follow me. Here," Bernard directed Voyd to a wheelbarrow parked on the carpet. The museum was hot as a steam-room. Voyd grabbed the wooden handles and pushed the Beatles. Bernard ran in front of Voyd, dragging what looked like Frankenstein and The Creature of the Black Lagoon. They followed the twisting red carpet past more tipping scenes. "This way!"

Sunshine glared in the opened exit doorframe. Voyd steered the Beatles into the alley where there was shade and plenty of company. Hopefully these four in the wheelbarrow would make it. Not all the wax museum stars fared so well. He couldn't recognize some of them.

They went back and forth as many times as it took to clear the museum. By then, Lloyd, the owner of the meat locker on the other side of the alley, had opened his doors. Lloyd told them he didn't mind storing the stars. They put as many as they could fit. Thelma Ritter was face-to-face with a 300-pound cut of steer.

Finally Lloyd closed the freezer door and announced, "That's it, we can't fit anymore." He took off his black-rimmed glasses and cleaned the frosted lenses.

They stood by the porthole window. Bernard said, "I don't understand what happened, every night I make sure the air-conditioner is on. And I never use the radiators, not even in winter." He groaned and rubbed his forehead, "I should've torn them out a long time ago."

"Sounds like sabotage," the butcher said.

"Yes! Yes, it does!"

Voyd reappeared. He held two last wax stars. "Is there room for these?"

The locker was crowded shoulder to shoulder. Behind that cold door, you couldn't fit the shadow of a ballerina. They would've turned to wax puddles if Voyd didn't come up with a solution. He couldn't hold down a job, but he was a whiz with ideas. He offered to take the two figures home. He had air-conditioning, they would be fine there until the museum wanted them back.

That's how Voyd Lewismeter, immigrant from Mars, ended up walking two more blocks home to Warbler Street, carrying Joan Crawford and Conway Twitty.

2
BLUNDER

Voyd Lewismeter is an unsuccessful Martian. He's doing pretty good as an American though. He arrived on the planet already employed, married, and lives in a hologram. He just couldn't make it on Mars. Nothing was going his way, it seemed hopeless, and finally he went to the migration bureau. A bright poster on the wall commanded MARTIANS GO TO EARTH. After a little conversation and not much persuasion, they signed him up for the third planet. They assured him, "You'll do much better there" and they set him up with a temp agency in an American city.

Every Martian migrating to America first had to prove they could work. That was a big part of the adjustment to their new life. Like any other foreigner, Voyd was tested with a series of American jobs. Once he proved himself capable, then he could join the ranks at MarsCorp. That was the goal. He was looking forward to that day.

His wife, Marjorie, was still at work as he struggled in the door with his arms full. He set their new guests in the late afternoon sunlight by the window.

He may not be bringing home the bacon, as the Americans say, but he was bringing home the wax.

With the two of them watching the sky like statues, Voyd went to the phone and called Mars. Sure, he lost another job, but he was feeling good. Soon his wife would be coming home to dinner and fascinating guests.

After entering a series of numbers on the rotary dial, he waited as the receiver clicked and reached for the fourth planet from the sun. It would take a minute or so. He took off his fedora, clutched the brim, and sailed it towards the hat-stand near the door. The hat missed the empty peg, hit the wallpaper, and slid to the floor. That was okay, that move took practice. Not everyone could be Gene Kelly.

"Hello," said the voice in the phone, "Identification please."

"This is Voyd Lewismeter." Those words were

in Martian, no point not translating, it would only sound like a bird warming up on a wire.

"One moment please."

So he waited a moment. He liked the look of the room's new occupants. They looked like they could talk and sing. What a stroke of good luck the wax museum disaster was.

"Agent Lewismeter?" the voice in the phone startled him.

"Yes, hello Mr. Narp."

Jark Narp was his probation officer. Voyd could picture him sitting at his desk on Mars, with a sheaf of paperwork, tapping a pen next to the latest job listing. "I already heard the news. You didn't do so well, did you?"

All that joy Voyd brought inside his room crashed underneath those words. "I'm trying my best."

"I want to get you placed with our organization. I really do. But we need to know you're up for it." Jark scratched a line through the last job description. "Need I repeat our mission? Everyone starts out with Earth jobs, so you get to know the people, the ones we'll be selling to. It's so easy, they're ripe for the picking, their minds are already there. Somehow they make it through a day. When they fall asleep, this world vanishes, they go into a dreamworld. Nothing is real, but it seems to be. Then that vanishes and they wake up, all so they can start over again." He laughed, "They're just along for the ride." His office chair squeaked as he put another cigarette in his mouth. "Anyway…" the sound of a match being struck. "Like I said, I spoke with the temp agency already. They're willing to give you another chance." He mumbled through the smoke 150 million miles from Earth, "I guess I am too."

3
The NEXT MORNING

It was warm the next morning, more than warm, it was hot. Marjorie had kicked the blanket off their bed. Like most Martians, they liked to keep their bedroom at a comfortable -100 degrees. This heat was more like Venus.

Finally, she ran a hand across her forehead to her hot antenna and she groaned, "Voyd!" She shook him. "Something's wrong. Wake up."

He tumbled out of a terrible dream and lifted his head. "What? Why's it so hot?"

"The heater. It must be broken. Go check the thermostat."

"Okay, okay." He sat up and his head spun like a kaleidoscope.

Marjorie stood with him. "I'm going to take a cold shower."

He padded across the floor out into the other room. Their entire duplex steamed like a sauna.

He had to lean on the wall, feeling across it in the dim light for the thermostat. Martians couldn't survive this sort of heat. His fingers drummed over the buttons. He couldn't believe it—the numbers read 110 degrees! Monstrous! Quickly, he stabbed at the reset function, activating the AC. Then he turned towards the window. There was a California morning out there waiting to be let in. He stumbled his way and nearly fell onto the dim blue shapes near the curtains.

Joan Crawford was a bent-over wretch, body melted in the velvet folds of her dress and costume jewelry. He cried out. Why had he set her by the radiator? Voyd could almost feel himself wilting from its blasting heat. He dragged the actress backwards, her shoe falling off, revealing a lumpen foot. "No!" he cried again. He dumped her against a chair and wrenched the window open. The other wax figure had fared better. Further from the source of the heat, Conway Twitty was standing in the corner like a question mark.

"Marjorie!" Voyd called. He heard the shower and ran to the bathroom. "Marjorie," he opened the door and the cool mist in the air was refreshing as the Arcadian gullies back home. He needed a moment to catch his breath.

She slid the curtain back, "What is it?"

Voyd told her about the scene in the other room. He was in no rush to go back to it, but he had to get ready for work. The agency was giving him another chance.

beneath the mirage

4
A FAMILIAR-LOOKING MAN

Half an hour later, after some marmalade toast and a couple cups of Postum, Voyd gave his wife a kiss and left their duplex. It shimmered around him, a Brooklyn brownstone, vintage 19th century. On the path to the sidewalk, he stopped and turned to admire it and to remind himself he needed to add some pigeons, ones that would flap over the laundry lines stretched taut to the tree, and land and bob about their home's phony stone ledges.

The hologram hovered over what their house really looked like. Beneath the mirage, the reality dulled—their duplex was half of a ragged two-story thing boarded over with gray vinyl siding. It was no wonder the Martian holograms were so popular, they sang all shapes and sizes and colors all down the street—who wanted to be seen living in a washed-up minor key? Voyd and Marjorie lived next-door to a blue cathedral. There was a dove on top of the steeple. A Martian technician installed that feature only last week. For a reasonable price. Voyd thought of getting one too. Wouldn't a dove look good on a brownstone?

When Voyd turned back towards the street, he was pleased with the sight of their neighborhood. There were magic-looking houses, Martian holograms, everywhere to be seen. Martian technology had the Americans spellbound. So far, the Earthlings hadn't learned to reverse-engineer the process. The Martians owned a monopoly. All Voyd had to do was master the simple routines of this new planet, fit in like a hand in a glove, and he could—he froze in his tracks as a memory of yesterday reappeared.

A familiar-looking man in a maroon uniform was kneeling beside the meter on the lawn. He was the same guy Voyd saw in the alley outside the wax museum when Voyd was hauling Joan and Conway away. At that time yesterday, Voyd was too busy for conversation, but he noted the man tinkering with the heat unit controls. "Good luck," was all Voyd had said, then Joan Crawford's jet-black wig hid him from sight.

Now on the edge of their sidewalk, wires hanging free from the fuse box for their duplex, Voyd viewed the repairman with alarm. "You again!"

The man looked at Voyd. He pushed back at the red cap above his eyes.

What was the connection? Voyd wondered—first the wax museum malfunction and then the same heatwave in their brownstone home. Was it an epidemic?

"What's going on?" Voyd said.

"We're doing a city-wide test."

"Of what?"

"Engineering, heating, I don't know."

"Well, you almost killed us! And Joan Crawford melted!"

The repairman said, "Who? Was she a witch?" It wasn't that strange a question. Witches were out there and every once in a while the newspaper reported someone throwing water on one.

"Nevermind," Voyd told him, "I have to go to work." Voyd knew it was really his own fault, he should have calculated the risk of putting Joan Crawford beside a radiator. With the repairman returning to his wires, Voyd finally read the back of the uniform. "Wait—you work for MarsCorp? You're from Mars?" Voyd laughed. "I am too!" He lifted his fedora to reveal an antenna. "I'm pretty new here, I'm still on reviewal." He chuckled, "Wow, what are the odds—another Martian. You ought to know better than to turn up our heat though, you almost boiled us alive."

"I'm just following orders." He may have been from the same faraway planet, but he was distant, more concerned with getting this job done.

"Okay, well, I guess I should get going." Voyd looked at the digital watch on his arm. "I'm running out of time. I don't want to be late for my new assignment. Maybe…maybe I'll see you at the company when I get approved." There was no answer. No wonder, Voyd supposed the unfriendly repairman was from the Hourglass Sea. That's how they were. Anyway, Voyd had places to be.

5

The WAR AGAINST the WAX MUSEUM

What was his job today? His temp agency Labor Now would give him the details. But he had to hurry. Earth time was something to get used to. They didn't have clocks on Mars, time worked itself out, it wasn't screwed to a wall or worn on an arm.

The path to the trolley took him past more holograms—a pagoda, a Mother Goose shoe, a rocket ship, a tall thin hotel in Amsterdam blue—sights he had grown used to. He was even accustomed to panic in the alley behind the wax museum. Another fiasco was in progress. Voyd used this alley to cut through to the boulevard but he was afraid to go in.

It was yesterday all over again, only with twice the commotion. The wax figures were heaped back in the alley, along with thick torsos of thawed meat, cow and pig, and in and out the door of the butcher shop Bernard and Lloyd brought more victims. Even from the distance of the sidewalk, Voyd could feel the kiln bleating out the open doorway of the meat locker. It was the ending scene of The House of Stars replayed, and this time it had taken the butcher's establishment with it.

Voyd didn't need to go any further to know there was nothing he could do to help. You couldn't pull the *Titanic* back with string. He got no thrill watching the disaster—the alley was clogged with it—besides he was late for Labor Now.

He had to step aside as a big red truck arrived. It turned into the alley, growling and hissing, and Voyd pressed himself back against the bricks to give it room. What a morning, he thought, and he still had a trolley to catch. The truck drove into the mayhem and braked.

No shortcut today. Voyd didn't want to step around those massacred bodies, the puddles and piles of them, or the slabs already gathering flies, it was too horrible. The shadow of Omar Sharif dissolved on the bricks. It wasn't difficult to conclude, whoever started the war against the wax museum had come back to finish it off.

Voyd had a feeling he knew who was responsible—he wasn't far from a clue—the wire spilled out of the circuit box like a signature on the wall.

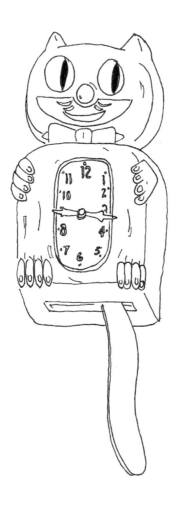

fame on the wall

6
EVERY MARTIAN'S DREAM

Voyd sat in a plastic chair and stared at the Employee of the Month. A framed photograph of Agnes Moorehead. A hologram of course, someone chose to look like that—and look what it brought them: fame on the wall. Voyd didn't expect to see himself up there, he didn't want to hang around here any longer than he had to, he just wanted acceptance by MarsCorp. It shouldn't take much longer.

And what if it did? When he reached the 25th mission, he would have completed his tour of duty, he could go back home, or he could volunteer for more.

The woman at the desk across from him set her telephone down and said, "Okay, Mr. Lewismeter. Thank you for waiting." She opened a file folder and flipped through the mimeographs. It was merely rote, she knew him well by now. Signs of concern began to form around her big glasses. She stopped reading and forced a smile. "You know, if you had been here on this time this morning, we could have placed you in a very fine job as a deckhand. As it is," she looked at the clock next to Agnes, "that ship has sailed. Literally. You can't catch salmon traipsing around on land."

"I know. I'm sorry, you wouldn't believe the way this morning began. I—"

"However," she continued, "I happened to be on the phone with a client who has an intriguing offer. How would you feel about working in a zoo?"

"Ohhhh," Voyd sighed.

"You're not making it easy for us," she said. That smile was taped to her face, all it needed was a flutter to fall off.

He pictured MarsCorp nestled in the woods on Jupiter Hill. The orange imported volcanic basalt stones reflected the setting sun. It was every Martian's dream and the zoo was just one more stepping stone to get there.

"Mr. Lewismeter?"

"I'd like that job very much," he said.

"Can you get there on time?" She turned to the

first page of the folder. "Our records indicate you have a car."

"Yes, we have a car but my wife uses it to get to her job in the valley."

"So you'd be relying on the trolley?"

"I'm in the market for a scooter, I just haven't got one yet. They're still a little out of my price range. Of course, a steady paycheck will remedy that."

She picked up a pen and crossed out 'car' on the first page. Then she wrote the address for his job on a canary-colored Labor Now notepad. "Be sure you're there tomorrow morning at eight sharp," she said as she handed him the torn page.

7

The WOLF at the ZOO

Sometimes he walked through Woodland Park, up the grassy hill and over the stone bridge raised above the road. A dirt trail ran past a silver chain-link fence that cut between the trees. On the other side of the fence was the zoo. He would stop beside it and be calm. Beyond the city sounds, the rush of cars and everything else, he would listen for animals. An elephant, a lion, the birds that were soundtracks in jungle movies. And every once in a while, he would see the wolf.

If it was there, it stood among the firs like a fairytale, staring back at him with golden eyes.

Can a Martian feel what a human can't, that unspoken field that surrounds something trapped? The zoo was like a radio channel, the air was filled with the sounds calling to Voyd.

What if he got some bolt cutters and cut a hole? What if the wolf snuck out the gap and was free in the city? The poor animal would be just like him, trying to get by. If it wanted to survive, it would have to be unseen, it would need to sense which way the woods were, miles past the concrete and traffic.

If the wolf was there, Voyd would do his best to communicate empathy. He would project a movie of the wide plains of Mars, the plateaus and peaceful hills and volcanoes where there were no fences and no zoos. If the wolf wasn't there, Voyd would hope it was doing okay.

Then he would turn around and cross Aurora Avenue again back to the grassy hillside. On mornings like this, on his way from Labor Now, Voyd decided to go see Marjorie. She was working tables at the café and she would tell him everything was fine, she would put her arm around him and he would feel better. She made him feel Martian again.

Voyd didn't want to report this morning to Jark Narp. Anyway, the old Martian would already know how he failed with another job—the woman at Labor Now was probably typing a report right now and sending it off to outer space.

8
DINOSAURS

One day, soon after he started Earth jobs, Voyd was a door-to-door salesman of bootleg movies. A man in a station wagon gave him a suitcase of videos to carry from house to house, to cover the York neighborhood.

It was fall. There were leaves on the sidewalk, yellow, orange, red, brown. He got to find pleasure kicking them, listening to their sound, watching them tumble. He saw schoolkids do it too. It was one of the many fun things they knew that the older Earthlings seemed to forget all about.

On Franklin Street, Voyd started at the house on the corner and worked his way down. Not everyone was home. Jobs took most of them away for the day. A dog would bark, a cat would sit in a window and stare. Someone old would cup an ear and shake their head and close the door. A couple times, Voyd opened the suitcase to show the video cassettes lining it, but nobody wanted any.

He guessed this was like fishing back on the Erythraeum Sea, on a bad day when nothing was biting, not even a shadow. A half hour passed, knocking on doors. He moved along the sidewalk skittering leaves. At Gladstone Street, he turned to the right and walked all the way to Iron Street. By then, his suitcase was a pound lighter, after leaving *Five Million Miles to Earth* and *The Three Stooges in Orbit* on the counter at Nelson's Market. That was a gamble. He asked if they would take them on consignment and the cashier agreed. It was a nice place, he thought about getting a sandwich. Maybe another time. When he left, he looked back. Sometimes you didn't know if you were walking into a hologram or not. They had no reason to hide what they were, an old wooden storefront serving the neighborhood since 1895.

Another block took him past Harriet Park. The tall trees were rattling their leaves in the breeze. He crossed the street and found a spot on the edge of a cold slide. The swings moved a little on their own. He took off his fedora and rubbed his head. He was the only one in the park, everyone was at work, or school, or in houses that didn't want videos.

His heavy suitcase was resting on the damp woodchips.

Jutting over Iron Street were sandstone outcroppings, looming like the backs of dinosaurs.

9

The FOSBURY BOY

The sun looked through the yellow leaves on Potter Street that day. Voyd failed to make any sales. There was an art to the sell, that's what they told him at the agency. If that was true, he stood on the doorstep of the Fosbury house with a handful of ruined brushes, dry paint tubes and a canvas that was torn in half.

A boy wearing pajamas slouched in the doorway and told him, "I stayed home from school. I told my mom I was sick." He grinned at that. "She believed me."

Voyd said, "Well, maybe you have some money of your own. Would you like to buy a movie? I'm sure there are some you'd like." He set his suitcase down on the step and fumbled with the latches.

The Fosbury boy said, "I saw you from my window when you were at the playground."

Voyd opened the lid and reached for *Robot Monster*.

"I saw your antenna, you're a Martian, aren't you?"

Voyd paused. Like most Martians, he tried to keep a low profile.

"How did you get here? In a rocket, or one of those UFOs?"

"No, that's a common mistake these movies make. It's actually very simple to visit another planet."

"Gee, would you show me?"

"No, I don't think so. If I told you, pretty soon there would be Earth people all over the universe."

"Aw, come on! I won't tell!"

"I'm sorry."

"Then I don't want a movie!" the boy pouted.

"I'm sorry, I can't say."

"Goodbye!" The boy slammed the door.

The little Fosbury sign stringed to a nail rocked back and forth.

Voyd shut the suitcase. He sighed. It was strange that people would order their days with jobs like these. On Mars everyone had a robot or a clone to do the dreary work for them. His feet

46

were sore, he hadn't made a dime, the car waited for him at the end of Potter Street. Here on Earth, in America, he had little time for the pleasures of a day, and by evening he would even be too tired for zarpek.

10
A PAPER BOAT

One good thing about that job, Voyd kept a video for himself. It could be said he stole it. His conscience didn't seem too worried and that may have been a character flaw, one that the agency would probably take note of. When he was sitting in Harriet Park that day, he wasn't just worn, he was thinking about an idea that came to him on the edge of the slide, an idea for a way out of all these jobs.

The cassette cover inspired him.

The Cosmic Man.

A white ball hovering in a California canyon.

A phantom from outer space.

A warning to the people of Earth.

As he watched the movie that night, he translated it into Martian, writing in a notebook.

Then he realized it needed something more, the story needed to be told in his own words. Voyd was no Edgar Ulmer, but the movie gave him the push to create for himself. He was surprised how easily the words came. It was a talent, like working a lathe, or loading a forklift, or gardening. And it came to him naturally, he felt part of a channel, a paper boat that flowed in a canal. It was too bad Labor Now couldn't source him into that.

By the end of the week, he was well on his way. He sent a chapter off to *Martian Adventure Stories* magazine. That's what writers do. He sent another chapter to *Planetarium Equinox*, others too. He told Marjorie, just wait, pretty soon I'll have published books. You'll see! He didn't tell Jark Narp—this didn't feel like a job, not yet, not until he could make a living from it. Then he wouldn't need MarsCorp. No more timesheets and timeclocks. He would be working in a world of dreams.

If it wasn't easy, that's how it was meant to be. The rejection letters didn't stop him, they blew through him like autumn leaves. It would look like another something he failed at, but it wouldn't be, would it? Adversity comes with the territory. There is no turning back. He was on his own. Listen up, Warbler Street, listen to your late-night bird as he clacks on a typewriter far into the dark, until finally, he gets into bed with his wife, sure that what he has done will be something all of Mars will enjoy.

11
BONITA

The Nimbus Restaurant is up on the 15th floor of the Bellwater Tower downtown. When the elevator door rolled closed behind him, Voyd looked for Marjorie. Across the room, he saw her by the windows, white apron tied in a bow behind, taking an order from two people at a table. It was the start of the lunch crowd and it looked like she was on her own, and busy. He didn't see Diane.

At first it crossed his mind that he could help. Once he played Martian harp for the diners, but the customers complained. Hands on ears! At least he had one fan, someone who told him, "It doesn't bother me. I've been welding sheet metal all day. I can't hear a thing." He could try carrying plates for Marjorie, refilling glasses, but he failed at that too, she would gently tell him she was doing alright alone. So Voyd went to the back of the room, grabbing a full dishtub on his way to the kitchen.

The radio played on the spice shelf. The cook was busy with a sandwich on the stove and Sunny Jim was at the sink, hands sunk in soapy water. He turned slowly like a stalk of celery as Voyd entered the room and set the tub down. A cigarette stuck to his lip burned with a thin trail of smoke.

"Hi Sunny!" Voyd greeted him. The old guy had been here longer than any cook or waitress. It wasn't hard to believe he came with the place, like the wallpaper in the dining room.

Sunny Jim removed a hand from the water and tapped his forehead in salute. Some bubbles stuck to his freckled skin and rusted hair. "How you doin?" he asked.

"I'm alright. Okay. I lost another job," Voyd shrugged.

"Yeah," the dishwasher nodded.

"But there's another one tomorrow." Voyd was going to tell him he was signed up for the zoo, but just then a pair of cool hands slipped over his eyes.

"Guess who?"

Voyd smiled. "Bonita Granville?"

Marjorie laughed, "Come on," she grabbed his hand and pulled, "I have a table for you, sit down.

I'll get you a Postum."

The sandwich flipped over the blue gas flame, bread turned golden brown. They left the kitchen and Voyd could have sworn they were together in those fields of Valles Marineris again. The chairs were stalks and the tables were humming flowers, red checkered petals catching the light of a distant sun.

Marjorie kissed him and gave him a spot by the window with a view of half the town. He was quickly entranced by the toylike layout of roofs and trees, the windup motion on the streets, colors and patterns, the clouds, the waves, the giant robot standing in the shallows of the bay.

12
JOB #17

After being a video salesman, Voyd was a robot repairman.

It began humbly enough. That morning at Labor Now they sat him at a table and gave him a shoebox. Inside the box were the tumbled parts of an alarm clock. He was timed to see how long it would take him to put it together. One minute thirty-eight seconds. Not bad. Martians were good at machines. But he knew it wouldn't be a factory assembly line job when they assigned him a hologram.

Voyd pinned the button to his coat and followed the receptionist to another smaller room. There wasn't much space in there, with the hologram ray and the lead shield he would stand behind. She showed the taped line on the carpet and told him to wait there, then she left the room. This was the first time he wore a hologram for a job. He guessed it must be something important.

He shut his eyes. He knew what was coming.

What he didn't know was who he would look like.

After a flash of light and the dying whirr of the Martian invention, he waited for the door to open again.

"Right this way, please."

A puff of ozone in the cramped room.

He followed her back to the office and she handed him a clipboard.

"Have a seat."

He sat down and examined the paperwork.

"That's you," she said.

Voyd looked at the rectangular photograph and gave a sort of laugh. The new him was familiar. He had seen that face in movies and at The House of Stars. Why him though? Voyd thought of changing it—he could click the hologram button until he found Gary Cooper—but if they checked up on him and didn't see his assigned role, he knew he'd be in trouble.

"Don Knotts," said Voyd.

"That's correct."

Before he left Labor Now for work, Voyd wore blue coveralls and a white backwards cap.

13
NIRVANA

Voyd sipped his Postum and stared at the robot landmark and remembered bringing it to life.

First, they put Voyd in the back of a van. It was a strange work crew, Don Knotts, and on the bench behind him sat Laurel and Hardy. There weren't any windows to see where they were going, the white walls were smooth as a seashell inside, and a curtain was pulled across hiding the driver and the windshield view. A murky light muzzled through the blue cloth. Voyd's senses were on alert, he could hear the radio playing faintly from the dashboard, the same country-western station the cook at the Nimbus listened to. He counted the turns they made—left, right, right, left, straight—like a blindfolded pigeon memorizing its path. On the backseat bench, Stan Laurel whimpered.

After nineteen more turns, the van stopped and the driver rolled the window down.

"JJ111," the driver said.

The guard or gateman muttered some reply. Voyd could also hear seagulls and smell the ocean and feel the pummeled drone of heavy machinery, forklifts, trucks, and the ceaseless pull of the moon. They were at the waterfront. Ollie said something soothing. When the van started forward again, the tires bumped them over the wooden joists of a pier.

Were they going to board a ship? At this point, Voyd didn't know. Why did they time his clock repair skills? Why did he need a disguise? He turned around to ask Laurel and Hardy if they had any clue, but he didn't have to—their hologram eyes were opaque in the gloom. They were always the victims of whatever was on the way, but it was comforting to know that whatever they were going to go through, they were going to survive.

The van entered a big warehouse. The gradient light in the back of the van changed from day to dark and then began to glow from the overhead fluorescence. The driver parked in a bright pool next to a hundred-foot robot, lying down like the Buddha on his way to nirvana.

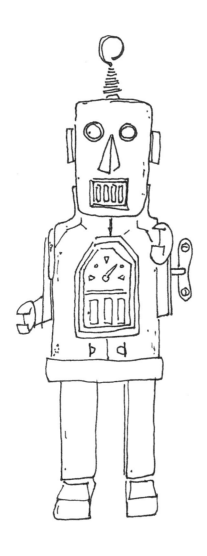

a gentleman from Harlem

14
WORKING

Voyd knew what he looked like, but he didn't feel like Don Knotts. He wasn't going to drop a wrench into the robot's works or knock a thermos of coffee into its circuits. He leaned over the open chest of the robot with his surgeon-like hands dug in. There had been some damage, mostly due to time, but he was doing what he could.

What about Laurel and Hardy? Why had Labor Now sent them along? Stan Laurel approached with a can of starter fluid he found in the van. "Will this help?" he asked.

"Give me that," Oliver Hardy snatched it from him. "I'll do the honors." Then he grinned at Voyd and cordially tapped the flammable can with a finger. He was a gentleman from Harlem, Georgia.

Voyd was busy with the clips on a distributor cap.

"Ollie…" Stan whimpered. He touched his partner's sleeve.

"Don't worry, Stanley, I know what I'm doing." Hardy gave the can a shake and pointed its nozzle.

Stanley squeaked as he watched the can spray into the robot's eye.

A lantern gleamed in it for a moment. Then the light died like an ember.

"Oh dear," Ollie said. He told Voyd, "I thought we had it going."

Voyd could tell why the robot wasn't working. He peered around in the hatch one last time. Wires were chewed through, the terminals were corroded, it was missing a spindle. He unscrewed a sparkplug. "We're going to need some new parts," he called.

They stopped work for the day. The van took them back into town. After sixteen jobs, it looked like Voyd was needed. That night he told Marjorie about his day. He was confident he could get the job done and it felt good that someone finally recognized his worth, especially once he got the robot functioning tomorrow.

Marjorie's eyes twinkled, "What if it calls for a robot revolution and all the machinery turns against us?"

"It won't."

"That's just the sort of thing that would happen in one of your sci-fi movies," she said.

"I know, but it won't be like that. This is just an old invention. We don't even have the parts for it, it might not work at all."

"I wish you'd be careful."

"I will," Voyd said, "I promise."

15
WISHBONE

It turned out to be simple. The next day, Voyd fashioned a stainless-steel part and put a new wishbone in the robot and it worked fine. It sat up, head brushed the suspended fluorescent lamps rocked on wires, arms pushing, knees bending, as it began to stand, rising like a chimney right through the roof, into the air outside. Voyd and the rest of the crew ran as sheet metal scales clattered down. Everyone was shouting, heading for the doors, while the hundred-foot robot Frankensteined ahead, cutting a path out of the old warehouse, leaving its silhouette behind.

Nobody knew how to stop it or what it was thinking or where it wanted to go.

A day later, they still didn't know, nor after a week or a month.

The robot wandered around the city. It changed places late at night or in the early dawn. You wouldn't think something that big could move so quietly, like the moon passing overhead. It slips between buildings, steps over telephone pole wires, parking lots and backyards, the culverts and hills. Sometimes it causes traffic jams, when it stands in the middle of a road, but people were quick to adapt. Every hour the radio would report where it was. Next to the monorail track, the salmon hatchery on Electric Ave, a copse of trees on Donovan, the school playground on 24th, tied with red and white balloons at a Safeway sale, planted in a vacant lot like a giant windmill. Once it got somewhere, it was there for the day. Like a living thing, it seems to need sleep or maybe it just gets tired and fancies a rest. Was it searching for something or lost? It was adapting, fitting in just like everyone else.

A rainy-day smoke-break at Job #21, on the loading dock of Linoleum Etc. The robot was only a block away. Shining water ran down its shoulders. Voyd listened to some crows. The guys clouding around on the platform were talking about the giant robot.

"We're lucky it isn't causing more trouble."

"What about Morton's? You see the mess it

made?"

"It can't go stomping around the city and not land on something."

"What if we trick it into walking into Green Lake? It might get stuck in the mud."

"Has anyone thought of asking it to shut itself down?"

"You want to tell a hundred-foot robot to shut itself down?"

That caused some laughter in the group.

What would these poor Earthlings do? Voyd stood in their smoke and wondered. He felt a little responsible for the way it ended up tied to the town.

16
MARJORIE STARS

It's true, once you start a robot like that you better know how to stop it too. Voyd never got the chance.

Marjorie could see him watching the waterfront. She knew what still troubled him. "You think it's your fault? It isn't. You're not a robot repairman anymore."

"I guess not." He sighed, "I don't know if I'll ever get hired for MarsCorp."

"Here," she refilled his cup. "Don't worry. You can get another job. You'll show them."

"I know." He took a sip. "You're right."

But his failure literally followed him around, all he had to do was see the robot to be reminded. It was a regular landmark like the Eiffel Tower or the Space Needle.

Marjorie gave his shoulder a squeeze. She would have got him a job at Nimbus, but she knew how that would turn out. *Martians Help Each Other*, was drilled into them when they came to Earth. No matter what happens, look out for one another. "I love you," she whispered.

"Thanks," he said. She was more comforting than anything in this world but when she left for another table, the Postum was all he had, cupped in his hands. And he couldn't help it, his eyes drifted back to the giant robot standing knee-deep in the bay. Every once in a while, the town would try a new way to defeat it. Boats were tied to its metal legs, churning at the water trying to pull it in. Voyd could see the white wakes plowing at the sea. It was pointless, you couldn't turn it off or knock it down. They would learn their lesson though. They would keep bothering it enough that it would wake up and lumber like a bear. It would pull those boats with it onto shore, over dry land, stones, grass, cement, across the parking lot and across Maritime Drive. A trawler would be dragged all the way to Magnolia before the captain could cut the line.

When Voyd finished his drink, he got a pen from his pocket and drew a heart on the napkin. He wrote Marjorie's name, with each letter surrounding it like stars. She would find it when he was gone and she would put it safe in her apron pocket.

17
HIDDEN TALENTS

"Did you know you have hidden talents?" The man in a canary feathered suit handed Voyd a card. "I'm Aloysius Roy. Have you ever acted before?"

Voyd read the card. "Talent scout?"

"That's right. I noticed you pouring Postum. You have a certain air. I happen to represent a director who needs a Martian."

"Really?"

"Sure," the man grinned. Voyd was reflected in his sunglasses, still looking astonished as the 1936 moment when Mervyn Le Roy discovered Lana Turner at the soda fountain of Top's Café. "Call me for the details."

Voyd was bolted to the 7-Eleven linoleum, watching Aloysius go out the glass door to his elegant ostrich rickshaw. It lurched, wings spread, and hurried away. Able to move again after finishing his paper cup, Voyd didn't bother with the payphone outside, he took off his fedora and contacted Marjorie by antenna. He watched the cloud geography while he told her what happened.

On the trolley home, he imagined himself in a sci-fi movie as a cruel Martian invader. They would put him in a space uniform, under green makeup to deliver his line, "The invasion must not fail." Some people did alright finding jobs in the *Herald*, at Labor Now, or word of mouth, but he was different, he knew it: he had star appeal.

At the studio the next day, he was made-up just like he predicted. His Martian intuition was right about that. He left the trailer wearing a phony costume and they leaned him against the counter in a diner set. Not very Hollywood Martian, the only saucers in the plot went under teacups. A woman held the script for him and showed him what to say and he couldn't believe it. Other actors took their places. Voyd had no problem memorizing his line, that wasn't the problem. It was the words. He knew if he didn't say it, they could replace him with a hologram. They preferred authenticity, he admired that, but what they were asking him to recite was something no Martian could ever say.

Could he?

With the camera rolling, he still didn't know if he could.

He held his breath as the jolly customers were filmed drinking coffee, laughing, chatting, while an orchestra played and an announcer intoned, "There's nothing as good as a cup of Luwak blended coffee." And then the camera froze on Voyd, with a mug held up in salute, as he said, "So good, even Martians agree!" That was it, Voyd's contribution to the history of film, a commercial for TV. It wasn't Jack Pollexfen, Voyd knew that. He was just glad the coffee cup was empty. Lana Turner got her break and became a movie star, that was one-in-a-million, Voyd decided for his sake he better stick to Labor Now.

18
The CHARO ANECDOTE

Labor Now sent Voyd to a bait shack just a few blocks off Boulevard Park. It sat between a galleon and a vacant lot. They weren't lying about their broken hologram, unless they wanted it to look like a bait shack. The sails rippled on the big wooden ship pulled ashore next to it. Voyd saw a real seagull fly through the top of the hologram. Birds didn't seem bothered with holograms.

Voyd read the words painted on the side of the small white house: *Live Bait and Tackle Shop. Minnows, fiddle crabs, fresh dead shrimp, mermaid.* Posts strung with rope guided him to the door. The Open sign rocked in the window as he went in.

The man at the register noticed Voyd's blue Labor Now windbreaker. "You the guy they sent?" Then he figured Voyd had to be and told him to follow him. "Problem is with an aquarium motor." He pushed on a turquoise door and they entered a back room that smelled like low tide underneath a pier. Pipes ran from the floor and fed water into barrels full of minnow schools and bubbling tanks of other baitfish, weeds and snails. The floor was wet with puddles, zigzagging pipes on the ceiling dripped, the room could have been a haunted submarine.

As soon as he stopped looking around at the fish on either side, Voyd saw where they were going and he noticed what went wrong. A familiar heap of museum wax blobbed next to a rocking chair. "Oh no," Voyd couldn't help saying aloud.

"Yeah," the owner agreed. "That used to be our mermaid." He touched the melted edge of her with a white sneaker. "She was our big attraction. You might have heard of her."

Voyd looked blankly at the scales and satin.

"Charo. Charo the mermaid."

Voyd asked, "Where did you get her?" though he already had a pretty good idea.

"Funny story. Let's just say I rescued her from a wax museum. Lots of people did."

"I know, I've heard."

"We kept her suspended in water on 80-pound test line. Before close, we take her out of the tank and put her in this rocking chair. Then we set her up for showbiz when we open. Not today though."

"How did this happen?"

"Terrorism! A guy came to test water levels and I don't know what else, and he left that electric heater on next to her chair. What for? I don't know. Does he hate mermaids? Don't ask me. It blew out our circuit too and knocked out the hologram. What a mess."

Voyd said, "I know him. He gets around." Voyd opened the fuse box. "I can get your hologram restarted. Sorry though, I'm afraid there's nothing I can do for Charo." She would need the divine guidance of a sculptor's hands, an alginate mold, surgical tools and layers of beeswax. It took Voyd less than five minutes tinkering to fix the hologram. When he left the bait shack and reached the street, he turned around so he could see what it turned into.

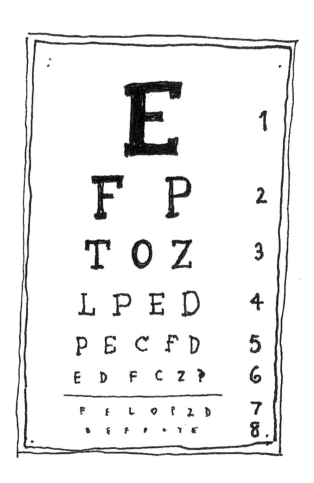

otherworldly letters

19
ALPHABET TROUBLE

It's not every day you find a book about Minta Durfee. Voyd tucked it under his arm, along with a mica page Martian edition of *How to Find Your Way Up the Ladder to MarsCorp*. It was advice for simpletons, rubes worse than him, who were struggling on Earth. He must have looked like one too—it was easy to go into a good bookstore and get lost, in fact it was the sort of lost he enjoyed—and a girl who was stocking a nearby shelf asked him if he needed help.

"Oh," he said, "I don't know, I guess so...or not. I'm having alphabet trouble. I'm just wandering."

She smiled. She didn't know much about Martians. The books they stocked for them weren't much help, shiny and soft with otherworldly letters that ran all over like startled birds. She knew a word or two though, everyone knew a few, and when she said it, she blushed.

Voyd knew what she meant, it wasn't easy for people to say, and he replied, "Good day to you too." He carried two books, one for Marjorie and one for him, and he might have gone to the register to pay, he was on his way, but he was stopped by a stack of paperbacks towering up from the floor. Placed on top he read the title *Red Mars*. That got his attention.

He found it amusing to read these old books about Mars from an Earthling point of view. Before contact was made and Martians began landing on Earth, all the imaginings were called science fiction. He found a place to put his books while he opened the paperback to a spot marked by a bookmark. This was as far as the last reader got, and they left a strip of gray paper. He turned the book so he could read what was scrawled on the marker. CIA-029 K48. The things people left in books were memorials to another time: trolley transfers, pressed flowers, receipts, grocery lists.

"Hey, I remember you," a voice shrilled.

Voyd almost dropped the book. Martians don't forget faces. The Fosbury boy he tried to sell a video to was staring at him.

The boy grinned, "Hey, is it true that Martians

only have one cuss word?"

"Yes, I suppose."

"Make him say it," Hollis Fosbury's friend urged, poking him in the ribs.

Hollis narrowed his eyes, "Can you say it?"

Voyd answered quickly, "No."

At that, Hollis kicked Voyd in the shin.

"Flimnap!" Voyd screamed in pain.

20
On the TROLLEY

Dusk was falling on the trolley as it turned onto the boulevard. Rush hour traffic, lights showing in store windows. Voyd was hoping to read about 1914 in the Minta Durfee book. He turned to the chapter titled "An Incompetent Hero" just as a man in a bright red knit suit stood up in the aisle. His bowtie was a felted blinking eye.

"Hello ladies and gentlemen and welcome to the 105, with service from here to there. My name's Derry. I'm more than happy to be your entertainment tonight. Thanks! Thanks for the applause. Thanks, take it easy, don't hurt yourself." The only sound around him was the trolley creak and rumble. "This is what I like, a captive audience." He stomped on the floor. "I understand they got the trapdoor fixed so I won't fall through." Someone laughed. Derry took comfort from that.

"Say, are there any Martians on board? I'm just kidding, I see one." He singled out Voyd. "What's your name, sir?

"Voyd."

"Voyd?" Derry grinned and scanned the faces, "*Voyd?* Really? You know, in our language a void is a vast empty space of nothing."

More laughter, some of it nervous.

"I'm just kidding, pal. You're okay. You guys beat us fair and square. I hope you're enjoying our planet."

Voyd answered him quietly, "I am."

"You left your ray-gun at home, I hope?"

More people were laughing. Derry pretended to point a pistol, hamming it up.

That was enough. Voyd pulled the cord and got off the bus as soon as he could. Hurt leg or not, he had enough. This sort of thing happened once in a while. On the job, at Safeway, taking a seat on the trolley. He was still a long way from Safeway and the wax museum and the alley to Warbler Street. He was sore when he got home, but Marjorie was there and she knew what to do. The next day his leg was better, bruised, it still hurt to walk, but better. Voyd wasn't taking any chances though. He stayed off the boulevard, stuck to the backstreets and alleys, avoiding any sign of the trolley, walking to another failed day at Labor Now.

21
In a BLACKBERRY RIVER

By not taking the trolley and walking instead, the planet took its time around him. There were things he missed about Mars, there was nothing quite like the windswept plateau of Tharsis Mon, but there was also beauty and mystery here in this city. The way to the Bird Streets was linked by tree-sheltered trails, meandering over ridgetops, stopping for pavement, starting again, winding past windows, houses, apartments, parking cars, curtained by leaves, a series of shoreline corridors and alleyways. If you weren't in a rush, holding a steering wheel or riding on tracks, you could find a whole other world.

After an old cedar fence, Voyd's path was bordered with piled high blackberries on either side, great waves of them frozen for this Martian Moses to pass between. Sparrows hopped around the bramble like minnows. Who knew if greater creatures lurked deeper in the shadows? Megatherium and glyptodons could be hiding unseen. Gleaning around the vines were blackberry pickers. They were all wearing the same Labor Now blue windbreakers. They moved silently along the thorns, they didn't need words, reaching in and out, just the patter of berries dropping in their baskets and buckets. It could be the sound of heavy rainfall.

Voyd walked past them. He didn't want to disturb their concentration. One dropped blackberry missing the bucket, bouncing off the rim, could start a whole avalanche. Someone would try to catch it, slip off their ladder and fall in and never be seen again. So Voyd passed by without a hello and turned with the green spiny bend of the path, like a leaf in a blackberry river.

The river ran out where it hit a sidewalk, tamped down by cement. Voyd stepped onto it and turned to the right. He lost the qualities of a leaf, he knew where he was going, headed for the neon sign atop a tall metal post.

Voyd had to circumvent a giant robot footprint left in his way. It was filled with deep muddy rain, lifeless looking water, no fish or lotus, almost a hopeless crater until the night came rolling in, dark and swayback as a bear sinking over the pond, and in time the universe began to appear twinkling in its fur. The first to form would be the little red headlight of Mars.

22
The MARTIAN DOLLAR

The Martian Dollar door hissed welcome as it opened and let Voyd enter the orange store within. Sand crunched underfoot. Every aisle was topped with candles. The scent was pleasant, the air was calm with recorded harp and the zither-like chittering of sand snakes. It was a tiny bit of home for those who wandered millions of miles away from it. That was certainly true for Voyd. There were circle-shaped landscapes of Mars hung on the wall like portholes, as if a different world existed outside, one more familiar and dearer than the rush of traffic on Fountain Street.

Hologram hands held out cans of peaches and Voyd stopped in the aisle to take one. What a treat that would be for dessert. Of course they were nothing like the peaches at Safeway. Sure, those American grocery stores were filled to the gills with packaged consumables but the whole endeavor seemed absurd to Voyd. On Mars he could just go outside and pick something to eat. He gathered the fixings for their meal from a slowly revolving display. Martian vegetables preserved better in a slow orbit.

He hummed along with the song, he couldn't help it, any Martian his age remembered it playing on the radio when they were young and far from Earth. It was taped to his memory like summer. It wasn't so bad missing out on another job. He was happy he would have a nice dinner waiting for Marjorie when she got home.

At the checkout counter, an Earthling and a Martian were talking. The old Martian woman, handkerchief on head, was holding a polka dot fruit.

"Shehvrraha," said the American girl. She wore a fake antenna on top of her hair.

"That's very good," the Martian replied.

Voyd settled his purchases on the counter and greeted them.

Another person leaned against the wall near a broom.

"Who's that?" Voyd asked.

The Martian told him, "Xavier Cugat."

"Or what's left of him," added the girl.

Voyd cringed. It looked like the bandleader had been torn apart by wild animals.

The girl said, "I found him on the way to work, in the alley by the wax museum. Someone chucked him out by the bins."

"What happened to him?" Voyd asked.

"What do you think?" the old woman said, "Someone tore out his heart."

Voyd shuddered. He quickly turned his attention elsewhere, to the top shelf behind the counter, out of reach, the zarpek kits in hot shades of red and orange.

23
WISH LIST

Voyd crossed busy Fountain Street and joined the treed path again. He wasn't far from the boulevard, it would have been faster to take cement, but he would never tire of funneling along these trails. Also, being unemployed, he had all the time in the world to marvel at them. A rain puddle fashioned like pewter slept across the gravel and as he crept around it, Voyd saw a Martian in it looking back at him.

A woman ran past him with a leashed dog trotting next to her. Voyd still wanted to get a pet Bleetnik. The Earthlings with their pets would be surprised to see a Martian dog, outrunning, outleaping, even flying. Also talking. There was nothing like a Bleetnik on this planet. Voyd had a catalog at home. The pages were marked with pets on his wish list. He could whistle a blackbird down from a traffic sign, but it couldn't float beside him and recite poems of the Phobos moon.

The blackberry pickers hadn't made it this far, tentacles with berries were waiting. Voyd plucked a few and enjoyed them as the path led him to the noise of cars and trolleys. He was back in American civilization. The dog with the jogger looked over its shoulder watching Voyd approach and stop at the crosswalk.

Voyd said hello and the woman asked if he had money for the meter. Voyd dug into his pocket and got a quarter. The dog watched him drop it into the slot machine mounted on the lamppost. The dial spun, round and round, and the arrow finally stopped on 10 Minutes. That was a long wait for the light to change.

"Flimnap!" Voyd cursed. He got another quarter and he got a worse result. "Forget it," he said, "I'll try a different traffic light," somewhere further from the trolley stop and the Safeway.

"Hold on," the woman said. "Do you have any more change? Let me try. I'm lucky with these."

She took his last quarter.

The dial spun again. Voyd was afraid to watch. His eyes followed the flyers taped to the pole, observing the stickers and the graffiti message:

CIA-029 K48.

The clicking arrow stopped, the slot machine gave a triumphant hoot, and the jogger clapped her hands. On the boulevard the traffic light turned yellow then red. The little green WALK sign on the other side of the road beckoned them.

24
The GIFT of LIFE

Voyd avoided the alley where the wax stars had met their doom. He wasn't ready to see half a Kitty Wells or someone even more desperate. He turned on Warbler Street and walked past the holograms. They formed dreams he wouldn't enter, spires and balconies and topiary, the cracked sidewalk was the only thing real.

He thought about nothing much.

Then he was in sight of the blue cathedral and the crooked aerials on the roof of the brownstone and another minute later, he was close enough to see someone crawling in their first-floor window. Voyd picked up the pace, he was almost running. "Hey!" he called as he passed the meter in his yard, "What's going on?"

Whoever it was, they seemed stuck. A toolbox was left in the grass below. The red legs of a work uniform kicked at the air. Voyd thought of

Winnie the Pooh caught in Rabbit's house. He also remembered the repairman who was here earlier this morning. "Hello!" Voyd called when he got near as he dared to those feet.

There was a muffled reply from inside the house, where the rest of the body resided.

"Oh, bother!" said Voyd. He realized he was talking to the wrong end of the repairman. He left the window and went to the door and the brownstone became half a duplex as he keyed his way inside to the sight of another Martian trapped in the wall.

"What on earth are you doing?"

The repairman blustered, "We know you have them." His hands scrabbled at the floor like lobster claws. The area rug surrounding the wingback chair had been pulled taught and crooked and out of reach. "I have my orders. MarsCorp wants them..." he puffed "...the wax dummies!"

That's when Voyd noticed Joan and her companion were missing. "They're not here..." He looked around the back of the chair then he left the room to go to the kitchen. Did Marjorie put them in there? No. He left and went up the steep stairs. The repairman called after him, but

Voyd wanted to check upstairs. No, he didn't see Joan Crawford and Conway Twitty anywhere. It's not like they could walk away, not in the shape they were in, and not without the gift of life.

Suddenly there was a cry for help from downstairs. Martians always respond to another Martian in need. Voyd clomped down the steps and back to his unexpected guest. The repairman had sunk some over the sill, a good push was all he needed to fall outside. He blubbered something as Voyd almost got to him before he was gone, slumped and dumped into the crackling rhododendron below.

25
MARTIAN INTUITION

Once he got rid of the repairman, Voyd called Marjorie at the Nimbus to see if she knew anything about Joan and Conway.

Marjorie knew right away. "I forgot to tell you, sorry. I brought them to the cellar."

"Why?"

"It's colder there. What if our heaters went on again while we were both at work?"

When he told her MarsCorp was looking for them, she was quick to decide that was it, whispering, "We can't have them at home anymore. Can we bring them back to the wax museum?"

"There's nothing left of it," Voyd said.

"I'll ask Diane if I can leave." Marjorie hung up and in fifteen minutes she was home.

Voyd was waiting for her with the two dummies wrapped up in blankets. Poor Joan Crawford was more of a ball. He heard the car pull to the curb and he was on his way. The duplex transformed as he stepped through it and rushed down the path away from the brownstone.

Marjorie jumped out and opened the side panel door so he could toss the bodies in back. As soon as he got on the front seat with her and shut the door, she sped the getaway car onto Kingfisher Street.

He answered her questions—fired off in quick succession as she steered—with the same "I don't know, I don't know," then he told her this wasn't the way this evening was supposed to go. He planned a Martian delicacy for her, instead of ghoulishly driving shrouded bodies to an abandoned building.

"I just think they're bringing us trouble with MarsCorp and we don't want any more of that. We can't have Martians raiding our house. Oh, I wish you never found those two. I should've known they were trouble." Marjorie slowed the car and turned into the alley. You couldn't ignore Martian intuition. It was always right.

There was just an ordinary alley scene awaiting them. Garbage cans, a pallet, a puddle that reflected the wires and the sky. The wax museum and the butcher shop had gone back to being doors in brick walls.

"This is it," Voyd said.

Marjorie parked the car half in the puddle, half on a cloud.

Voyd got out and knocked on the metal exit door. By the time Marjorie joined him, he knocked again and the door opened to a dim pumpkin light and the smell of crayons.

Bernard looked like the wind had gone from his sails and he had been floated aimlessly and shipwrecked and poured onto the sand. He stared at the alley with blank eyes.

"Hi Bernard," said Voyd. "We wanted to return your sculptures." He pointed at the car. "Joan Crawford melted."

"We still have Conway Twitty though," Marjorie said, "But he got a little crooked. We call him Conway Twisty."

"I don't care anymore," Bernard said, "I don't want them. I'm done with wax. I sold off everyone I had."

"What happened to the rest of them?"

Bernard shrugged. "I sold them to a Martian. He put them in a big truck and drove them all

away. I don't know why. You tell me. What's a
Martian want with my melted wax museum stars?"

26
UP and OVER

"We're not bringing them home." Marjorie was firm about that.

"Well, we have to put them somewhere. Somewhere safe. Besides, something's going on. I think they might be valuable." Martian intuition told him so.

Their little car puttered here and there for a while before a destination occurred to Voyd. Dusk was falling over the city, the streetlights were going on and Mars was an undimming nightlight far-flung in the sky. They parked in the shadows of Woodland Park.

"Oh, Voyd," Marjorie worried. "This isn't going to work. Someone will see us."

Carrying two covered bodies, one not more than a big beachball, across the lawns and dandelions bunched for night, hupping uphill to the pedestrian bridge that loomed over Aurora

Avenue—like ghosts they somehow made their way undetected to the forested edge of the zoo.

"This is your idea of somewhere safe?" Marjorie asked. She leaned with Joan Crawford against a tree. "Are we going to toss them over the fence?"

"No, no. Let me see…it's so dark…I know it's somewhere near." He set Conway Twitty beside her.

"Where are you going?"

"I'll find it, wait right here." And off Voyd went, cracking branches and stirring leaves underfoot. The sound of him faded. It was time for moonlight and the faint breath of the wind.

Marjorie was alone with two lifeless bodies. She had seen Voyd's black and white movies, she felt like one of those women who was about to meet a gorilla climbing out of the dark. This was the place for it, there were plenty of wild beasts close-by. A cage could have been left unlocked. A leopard could have got out. That could be it approaching, snapping a twig beneath a claw. Why were Earth women always in danger? "Voyd?" she called. She had Joan Crawford held in front of her, ready to throw.

A Martian silhouette appeared and Voyd said, "I found it." He slung Twisty to his shoulder. "It's the perfect hiding place. Follow me."

"How did you find it?" she asked. She was careful not to drop the great ball of wax in her arms. "Why are you wandering about the outside of the zoo?"

He laughed. "I'll be inside of it tomorrow. Thanks to Labor Now. Look—there it is."

"Where?"

"That tree. It's hollow."

"On the other side of the fence?"

Voyd set his statue against the chain-link and placed Joan with it. He motioned his arm, "Up and over and into there," he said. He held out his hand.

Marjorie locked her hand in his and they closed their eyes.

On Mars that's why people got married, to move the world in ways one person never could.

the usual fedora

27
LED to the ZOO

It was too bad they couldn't manifest another car. They were only able to make one appear and it took a lot of effort to get that. When they tried again later all they got was a bumper. Voyd dragged it to the backyard and left it under the tree, disguised as a park bench. Marjorie drove their car to work so that left Voyd to his own devices— either the trolley, or a long walk, or on a sunny morning like this one, two wheels.

How can a Martian scooter be described? Somewhere between a flamingo and a dandelion stalk on a windy day. In any case, Voyd couldn't afford one yet, so he put a hologram over a Schwinn. Parking at the 7-Eleven he could see the scooter's reflection in the big window. His own reflection wore a green suit, tie, and the usual fedora, all real.

A bird-like greeting chirped as he entered the store. "Good morning," Voyd raised a wave to the counter. Voyd was in a good mood. He was looking forward to his new job at the zoo. This was it, he could feel it, everything led to the zoo. Ever since he landed on this planet, he could relate to the Earth animals.

Along the wall to the left was a coffee machine and another pot next to it for Postum. Voyd could tell how many Martians came for Postum by the burned dark pour that filled his paper cup. He could have been the only customer in days. That was alright, he was still smiling. He was thinking of Marjorie. He couldn't wait to see her again. As he replaced the Silex on the burner, some drops spilled on his shirt cuff. He dabbed the stain with a napkin. It was okay. Nobody would notice. He pressed a button cufflinked to his sleeve and a hologram covered the stain. Martians thought of everything.

And he still had time! He stood in front of the 7-Eleven next to his scooter while he finished his drink. Did anyone else ever take a moment like this to enjoy watching the slow start of the day? The planet tipped and turned around the sun like a miracle, with blue sky, clouds, and look—people were too busy driving, riding trolleys, and running off to rooms.

Always looking more or less in tune with time, Voyd finished the last sip and crumpled the cup. Next stop, Labor Now. And then the zoo! He reached into the scooter mirage and grabbed the bicycle handlebars. If he got a chance during the day, he would stop by the wolf pen and make sure their old wax roommates were okay. At least they were safe in there, watched over by wolves.

28
The SMOKING HAND

Voyd was Don Knotts again. Either the Martians were getting lazy handing out holograms or this was a trusted all-American character. Voyd wore the strange mask, staring at the different hands that held the timesheet and pen and signed his name.

"Alright," the secretary took the paperwork from him. "You're all set. There's a car waiting to take you to prison."

"What? Yesterday you said I was working at the zoo."

"No, I'm pretty sure I said prison." She stood up and took the papers with her to a tall file cabinet. "You better hurry though, they're not going to wait all day, they're expecting you."

"Prison?" Voyd garbled. "What's happening there?"

She put his timesheet in a drawer and didn't

seem too concerned. "Search me." Then she laughed and corrected herself, "Search you!"

Earth humor. He considered abandoning the whole enterprise. His so-called scooter was tied outside, he could hop on and be gone. He could ride downhill to the sea. The day belonged to the free! He could easily spend the day on a dune or a stone, calling the seals. One time he got one to leave the water. It inched over the shore. Was it attracted to his Martian singing? Did they share a language? Was the ocean like outer space?

"Mr. Lewismeter?"

"Okay. I'm going." The office carpets, desks and chairs, dissolved into sunshine.

A dark blue sedan waited for Voyd. The engine muttered. The driver's hand, resting on the steering wheel, held a cigarette. The smoke drifted over the dashboard. Voyd paused as he read the word stenciled on the door in dull gold letters: REFORMATORY.

The smoking hand in the car window beckoned him. Voyd had to walk past his bicycle to get there.

29
WHISTLING

Did they really believe he was this Don Knotts person, Voyd wondered. Of course not, the whole world knew about holograms, they knew he wasn't real but part of them went along with it.

"This way, Mr. Knotts."

Another officer opened the iron gate, nodded, and gave him a brief smile as he stepped through the doorway.

It was a strange place for a Martian. Cages went up five floors and all along the walkway they passed bars with people cramped in cells.

"Keep it down!" growled the officer in front of Voyd as the chatter and catcalls began.

"Hey Barney," a prisoner hissed, "Did you bring the key?"

Someone started to whistle and before Voyd and his escort had gone another twenty feet, the same television theme song was picked up and turned into a chorus all around him. The noise was turning into a cyclone and the officers barked into it, but it didn't let up. They quickly escorted Voyd through the next locked door into an empty stairwell. The steel door shut behind them. The whistling scrawled on the other side as Voyd went downstairs. Their footstep echoes filled the stairwell, the whistling jeer faded.

A wall camera in a wire ball turned to follow them as they descended. Don Knotts was no stranger to being filmed. They stopped at the basement level. More keys jangled until the right one was found and scratched at the lock.

An officer said, "You ready for the dungeon, Mr. Knotts?"

Voyd's eyes went wide as saucers and the officers laughed.

The door opened to an underground factory and they had to give Voyd a push. He staggered forward. It wasn't his first job in a factory, he worked assembly lines before, loaded forklifts and pulled pallets back and forth. Only here, none of the factory machinery was working. A museum silence, except for a prisoner in a blue uniform, moving back and forth with the same monotony of a machine, hushing the cement floor with a push broom.

"Over here, Mr. Knotts."

They took him along a conveyor. The belt was still. A row of license plates were lined up in rows.

"We want you to take a look at the stamper. See if you can get it running again."

Another repair job, thought Voyd. That's what they want me for. He could repair a clock in seconds flat. A talent that came from the stars. If you have a giant robot that needs to run, hire a Martian for that too. They gave him a wrench and a screwdriver and it was up to him.

30
SIRENS

Voyd found the problem right away. A license plate was jammed in the gears. It wasn't difficult to remove the plate. It could be twisted free. CIA-029 K48. He set it aside and reattached the power cable. "Would you like me to start it running now?" he asked.

"Give it a go."

Voyd pressed the green button, a circuit blew with a bright snapping flash and the stamper shuddered. Then a pivot arm kicked out at Voyd and knocked him backwards against a pillar. He lost his breath for a moment, along with something else—his hologram disguise. The device attached to his nametag was shattered. No more deputy sheriff uniform, no utility belt, no more visored cap—Voyd wore his green suit, with his fedora on the floor. He groaned. It took an effort to breathe again, slowly reaching for his hat.

"Who are you?" a guard seized his arm.

"Martian," the other officer pointed at Voyd's antenna.

"Who are you?" the guard repeated, getting angrier.

Voyd told him, "It's still me. I just can't get myself back the way I was."

That was it, he couldn't even replace his fedora before he had his arm cuffed to the pillar. Voyd stood still while they tried to figure out what to do with him, a tense walkie-talkie conversation, discovering the door wasn't opening, green generator lights shined from the ceiling. Voyd answered their questions, no he wasn't a saboteur, and yes, he had been approved, he was a registered worker from Labor Now. They could call and find out. He let them react to the situation, he was tied like Odysseus to a mast, he could hear the sirens, but he couldn't move.

"Brother..." someone said. The broom sound had stopped.

Voyd turned and noted the small prisoner squinting at him.

"I'm a Martian too." He tapped his blue cap as if an antenna was underneath. "You gotta get me out of this place. Remember the Martian oath?"

Of course he did. Voyd had no choice, he had to uphold it. It only took him a moment to come up with a plan. He removed the cufflink hologram from his sleeve and programmed it with a word. "Here," he said. "Stand by the cement wall and put this on. You'll look like part of the wall."

The prisoner grabbed it.

"Oh," Voyd kept his hand held out. The coffee stain reappeared on his shirt. "Could you pass me my hat?"

"Sorry, brother," the grinning fellow replied. "I got to go."

31
ANOTHER DON

After everything was explained, Voyd was escorted very somberly from the prison. He apologized about the confusion and the stamper machine. No reply. They didn't give him a car ride back to Labor Now. They pointed across the yard where he had to wait at the bus stop with another prisoner, recently released.

Voyd turned from the road and watched the guards return to the prison. He thought about the Martian he helped in there. There was a lot of cement in that place, he could move like a checker piece from square to square. How long will a hologram last? There's no way of knowing for sure, hopefully long enough to follow the walls out.

"You got a match?"

Voyd shook his head no. The first four words this guy said leaving jail and Voyd couldn't help him. If this was Mars, you could use a clover twig scratched across a stone. It didn't look like he had much of anything, he only carried a plastic bag tied into a knot like a bindle. He had bus fare though. A complimentary token, care of the state. Voyd had one too.

When they got on the bus, Voyd found a seat in the middle, next to the window. It was a long ride. Lots of stops. The old man in front of Voyd was slumped against the glass. Sleeping? Dead? There was something funny about him, Voyd figured. It was another Martian intuition. The next time the bus slowed in the traffic, Voyd got up to investigate.

Just as he expected. The pin on the old man's suit said Labor Now and under that a name: Don Pardo. The bus shook and Voyd took the seat beside Don Pardo. Don was deep asleep. He must have had a helluva nightshift job. Poor guy, Voyd thought.

Then Voyd had a devious thought. A human thought. It was bad enough that he lost another job, he didn't want to show up at Labor Now with a broken hologram tag. Nobody was watching. Voyd took Don's pin, put it on his own green suit, and stuck Pardo with the broken one.

It was bad behavior. That wouldn't happen on Mars. Voyd's smile vanished. He looked at the undisguised person next to him, a man in his sixties with hands gnarled together. A herringbone flat cap, torn plaid coat. Crunched against the window, he would sleep for another hour and wake up lost and look around and see his own reflection in the glass.

Voyd got up and sat across the aisle.

He fiddled with the hologram settings. He turned the smallest spindle until it stopped on Don Knotts.

32
FLICKER

"Don! Oh Don!"

That was Voyd's hologram name. Even though he would soon be stepping out of it and leaving it on his peg in Labor Now, hung on the wall like an old comfortable sweater waiting for tomorrow, the name followed him outside.

Laurel and Hardy waved at him from the parking lot.

Voyd waved back. He turned on the last cement steps of Labor Now and walked towards them. Their black bowler hats, their familiar smiles— no wonder holograms had become so popular, they could put you at ease right away. They were standing by an Econoline van. One of the side doors was open.

"We really got into a fine mess with that robot, didn't we?" Ollie asked.

Voyd automatically searched the skyline. You

never knew where it would be. He agreed. He wished there was something they could do, but it seemed to be something people were getting used to. It stomped around and stopped.

Stan and Ollie invited Voyd to tea. That seemed like a good idea. It seemed like something they did often. The back of their van was set up like a home. Ollie took the teapot off an electric hotplate and Stanley carried three cups and they went through the parking lot to a tall hedge of juniper. On the other side was a lawn. It rolled gently downhill towards the green rooftops of the hospice.

They couldn't be seen, they were in a good spot, under tall trees, sharing a stone bench screened by blackberries. This would be a peaceful spot for someone from the hospice whose time was running out.

Stanley said, "We have a new job that starts at five."

"I just lost mine," Voyd said. "Again."

"You can't stop trying," Ollie nodded and sipped his tea, pinky held out.

Typecast as Laurel and Hardy—Voyd had to admit the Martians or Labor Now really were getting lazy with their holograms. Even if they had not been very helpful with the robot, Voyd liked Laurel and Hardy. Or whoever they really were… He was finding out. Every minute or so they would flicker, first one then the other, and in that instant Voyd could see a man and a woman who lived day-to-day in their car. Also, he could see through their bowlers, no antennas, they weren't Martians like him. Labor Now wasn't an initiation for them, they didn't get an American certificate, a home, and a luxury job at the Martian factory. They were doing this to survive.

33
The MARTIAN MACHINERY

There's a time every night when the holograms momentarily go off. It happens between 2:30 and 3. One moment the lights in the neighborhood are glowing like mad—Ferris wheels and windmills, the old-fashioned gas lampposts, the IHOP, totem poles, every castle, church tower, ziggurat—then like a switch being pulled, everything is gone. If anyone happens to notice the holograms wink out of sight, who would believe the story, coming from the sort of 2 AM wanderer nobody would believe anyway?

When the Martian wires and circuitry holding everything together stops, moonlight shows things as they really are. A black night sky background of stars, planets, and satellites. A luminous Milky Way appeared over the unprojected town. The moon made shadows on the Bird District and shines on the threadbare tiles of a roof on Warbler Street.

An alarm clock ticks beside the bed. Voyd and Marjorie are sleeping in their half of the duplex on the second floor. Their window glass shines with moonlight. Finding a spot where the curtains don't cover, Mars peeks in.

The clock numbers shimmer green radium. 2:22. Tick, tick.

After a couple of seconds, the Martian machinery kicks in again and the holograms are back, the black sky becomes cloudy purple. Voyd put his arm around Marjorie. He fell asleep holding her. She is dreaming she's working at Nimbus. Carrying plates. The robot was looking in the window. She stopped and listened. It was delivering a message from Mars.

34
EXTRAORDINARY

Jark Narp rested on a spoil of war: a fainting couch from the Palace of Versailles. Carved, gilded frames, horsehair stuffing, upholstered in red tapestry fabric. He was living the part. He took a sip of refined Postum. "How's that cebreniac working out? What's his name...Voula?"

"Are you referring to Voyd? Voyd Lewismeter?"

"Yes, of course I am! What's the latest?"

Narp's secretary ran a report. The computer screen in front of him fluttered. "It isn't good, sir."

"Well lay it on me, Anthrab! Surprise me!"

"His appearance at a prison resulted in him freeing a felon."

"What? Who?"

"A prisoner claiming to be a Martian."

"Oh for Bremms' sake!"

"Indeed," Anthrab nodded.

"Was it discovered?"

"No sir."

"Well, that's good!"

"No sir. It isn't. They might not know about the jailbreak, but they found another fault in Voyd's performance."

"Now what?"

"The prison released him from service for impersonating Don Knotts."

"Who's that?"

"Apparently an American sacred cow."

Jark Narp shifted. His orange toga sleeve flowed over his face like seaweed in a tide. "Well, I'm reaching my limit. How many chances do we give that guy? It's extraordinary."

"It *is* extraordinary, sir."

"You're telling me!"

The Martian headquarters was a hundred feet underground, beneath a crater planted with gorse.

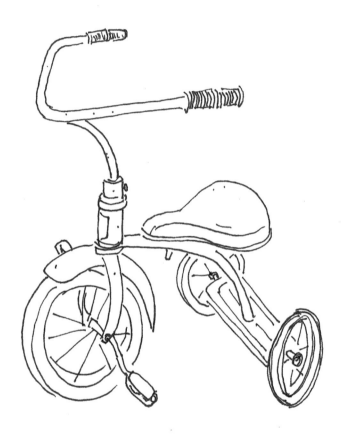

sent riding there

35
BETTY GRABLE

The next morning, Voyd was back at it, a new assignment at Labor Now, sent riding there on a trolley to an observatory job. It should have been easy, it was right up his alley. Up on Jupiter Hill, the white dome gleamed in the early sunshine. The trolley lurched and shook as it joined the tracks switchbacking up the steep climb.

Voyd was having trouble with his hologram. The nametag he had taken from the poor human on the bus yesterday was misbehaving. Don Knotts kept turning into Don Pardo. Voyd would reset the image, it would last until it didn't. It was frustrating. He spent most of the scenic ride tampering with the switch.

Then he had a little more trouble getting off the bus.

As Voyd reached the steps to the open door,

the driver grabbed Pardo's sleeve and said, "Hey buddy. Not so fast. I didn't notice you get on. The fare is two dollars."

Voyd explained that he was a hologram. A broken hologram.

"Nothing doing. I need two bucks. This trolley doesn't run for free."

Voyd pressed the stubborn button on his Labor Now tag, "I promise you, I paid when I got on. Do you remember Don Knotts? That was me!"

"Sure pal, and I'm Betty Grable." Still gripping Voyd's sleeve, the driver held out his other hand. "Two bucks or I call the cops."

"Flimnap..." Voyd sighed. He dug his wallet from his suit jacket and paid the man.

After those theatrics, was it any wonder that Voyd entered the observatory an angry Martian? He started on the wrong foot, with what employers like to call "the wrong attitude." And it was a simple job too, fixing the telescope in the planetarium was something he could have done in his sleep. It was just the state of his mind that caused him to pause while he was up on the ladder next to the lens. Nobody was watching him as he tore a button off his green suit and placed it on the glass. In the vast sea of outer space, it would look like a verdant planet had come into view. Just wait for the night, when the planetarium's great bronze shutter doors slid open to view the cosmic sky.

36
THEIR WINDOW

Saturday morning was a relief from Labor Now. Voyd walked into the soft daylight of the kitchen and started hot water for Postum—on Mars he would dip a silver ladle in the aqueduct, here he used a faucet—and rubbing his face and yawning he nearly blindly navigated their living room and opened the front door to get the newspaper.

Sometimes the paper didn't make it through the hologram. Sometimes it was thrown on the lawn near the whirligig. Today it died like a pigeon against the door. Voyd leaned over and got it, lifting it and removing the rubber band and unrolling the scroll all in one ballet motion.

The *Herald* headline read: NEW PLANET DISCOVERED. He stood there in the doorway in his bathrobe and laughed. Voyd couldn't help it. He read a little more about the beautiful, unspoiled green world and he chuckled. He knew what he had done was self-sabotage, but it was a joke, wasn't it? Maybe so, but Martians weren't supposed to do that. That was human behavior. He was picking it up.

Okay, he thought, his coat was missing a button now, but it was worth it. Wait until I show Marjorie the story. Then he heard a thump around the corner of the house. His smile flattened. He left the cement doorstep to see what it was. Under the rope running to the tree, their Martian clothes were drying in the sun. If anyone was watching from the street, they would see a well-dressed man rounding the grounds of his brownstone.

The leaves of grass tickled his bare feet. Not for long, he was there in a few strides, the west side of the duplex.

"Oh no…" Voyd gasped, "Not again." A pair of feet were kicking their vain way into the house, someone was stuck in the window. This time the legs weren't wearing the red uniform of the Martian repairman, and they were shorter too, blue denim cloth, with black shoes that had seen some wear. "What is going on?" Voyd sputtered. Was this the latest fad? Was their window so irresistible that people were drawn to it like moths on a summer night?

close enough

37
The MARTIAN LOYALTY OATH

The escaped prisoner tasted the Postum in his cup and made a sour face, "Ugh!" he cried, "What is this?"

Voyd looked surprised, "Postum, of course."

"I hate it," he pushed the cup away. "Don't you got any coffee?"

"Coffee?" Voyd repeated. Was he joking?

"Instant is fine."

"Coffee?" Marjorie gasped. She motioned for Voyd to join her in the kitchenette. Close enough to whisper, she got right to the point, "I don't think Wilby is a Martian."

"What?"

"Oh, come on, Voyd. He doesn't like *Postum?*"

"Well—"

"He asked for *coffee*," she hissed.

"It seems strange," Voyd conceded. "It does indeed. But maybe being in prison, he got used to coffee." He shuddered. "It's a terrible place."

"Fine." She turned to the stove and used the spatula to pry two sizzling discs onto a plate. "We'll see how he does with these pancakes."

"They look delicious, dear," Voyd smiled.

She took the plate around the counter. "Sorry, Wilby. We don't have any coffee," she announced. "I made you a Martian favorite though."

He glanced at the plate she delivered. Wilby had been on the run since his hologram cut out. When that happened, he couldn't blend in with the cement anymore, he was wearing prison blues. "How about you give me some different clothes," he asked Voyd.

Voyd set a bottle of Clorox next to the pancakes.

"What's that for?" asked Wilby.

"For your pancakes," Voyd said.

"Are you crazy! Pancakes?" He poked at one with a spoon. "What are these made of?

Marjorie crossed her arms. "Salt, magnesium, iron, with flour ground from the gullies of Sirenum."

"The best!" Voyd touched Marjorie's shoulder.

Wilby pushed his plate away. "Look, sister. I'm hungry. I haven't had food in two days, but I can't eat this."

"Bleach?" Voyd offered.

"No!" Wilby barked. It looked like he'd rather eat the tablecloth. Then he calmed himself. "Okay, you got me. I'll be honest with you, you're good people, Martians I mean…I'm not from Mars."

Voyd was stunned. Marjorie nodded. She had an intuition.

"When I heard about the Martian Loyalty Oath, I figured I could use that to my advantage. It worked. You got me out of the clink. For that I'm grateful. And thanks for your hospitality too, ma'am." He stood. "But I got to go."

They couldn't feed him, but Voyd gave him clothes and some money and told him where 7-Eleven was. The coolers were stocked with sandwiches made by Earthlings. There was coffee brewing. Voyd still felt responsible for Wilby even though Wilby wasn't Martian. Marjorie felt something less. They watched Wilby go to the door in a set of Voyd's clothes.

Saturday shined in. Wilby tapped his fedora and shut the door behind him.

The room was quiet and they were alone.

"Wow…" Marjorie finally said.

38
STERLING HAYDEN

After their pancakes and Postum, Marjorie and Voyd left their hologram. He held her hand, they still did that, after all the years. An imaginary cow watched them from the neighbor's yard. Oatmeal Houston lived next door in a ranch house. Right now he was on Saturday morning TV pushing cereal between cartoons. "This is Oatmeal Houston for Open Range Oatmeal. You like it? Sure you do! Everyone loves it." Once in a while he would ride a horse, back and forth in the pen, but if he stepped beyond the split-rail fence, the illusion would fail, he would be seen holding two coconuts, clapping them like hooves as he set foot on the sidewalk. Oatmeal in baseball cap and old sweater. The cow's big brown eyes watched them pass.

On Saturdays they visited the Martian Conservatory.

They headed for the trolley stop on the boulevard and Voyd figured it was fine to take the alley shortcut. Why not? Days had passed since the wax museum melted. Alleys held on to the past. The same puddles would stay in place for years. You could spot appliances and mattresses that looked like they'd been abandoned since 1982. You could stand on the hill and look down the alley with its ceiling of sky held up by bent telephone poles receding into perspective. One of those poles leaned against the bricks. A wanted poster of their breakfast visitor was stapled with the other scraps of paper.

Marjorie said, "How long do you think it will take them to catch Wilby?"

Voyd shrugged.

"I hope he doesn't rat you out as an accomplice. That's what happens in those movies you like." She said it with a gleam in her eye, Voyd knew she didn't believe those movies were anything more than dreams. That possibility of prison hadn't occurred to him though. What was the penalty for hologramming a felon? "Oh Voyd," she squeezed his hand. "Don't worry. You're not George Raft."

"Yeah," he replied. He tried to look like Sterling

Hayden.

Marjorie laid her head on his shoulder as they walked into the alley.

It wasn't much further, on the other side of a dumpster close to Lloyd's empty butcher shop, when someone begged rapidly, "You want to buy some quality used bacon?"

Voyd held up his hand like a stop sign and said, "No." He wasn't fond of this planet's food. Wilby's reaction to their Martian fare revealed the feeling was mutual. For Voyd, maple syrup poured on pancakes was as incomprehensible as Clorox.

Marjorie looked over her shoulder. "He wanted us to buy used bacon?"

"*Quality* used bacon, I think."

"That seems strange."

"It *is* strange," he agreed.

Along the brick wall, the butcher shop door was padlocked. They read the sign taped to it. For Sale by Owner.

"The wax museum is for sale too," Marjorie said.

Sterling Hayden shook his head in disbelief. What was wrong with the world?

39
NEAR ZEPHYRIA

There weren't that many Martians in town, but they would congregate at the conservatory every Saturday the way churches would open for business on Sundays. The huge glass greenhouse reflected the dull colors of the apartment towers and warehouses around it. The Martian engineers had recreated the ornate design of the Victorian era, setting it carefully on the paving of America like a crystal treasure. An orange light throbbed from inside, sometimes winds would blur the glow with dust.

Marjorie and Voyd had a favorite bench near Zephyria, with Electris in view just beyond the craters and Cimmerian Sea. "Look!" Voyd pointed at the distant clouds raised by a herd of Semi-Sentient Speedbumps. Marjorie had her shoes off. She wriggled her toes in the sand.

40
The AL PACINO POSTCARD

Their next stop was the pier, a couple hours later. People walked by them with their dogs. Voyd thought about the one he wanted to order from Mars. When they took it to the boulevard, he could toss a thyle and their dog would soar out past the railing, kicking its legs in the air like an eggbeater. Voyd leaned on the railing and looked twenty feet down into the green water. He hoped to see a slow Xiphactinus swim along the pilings, big as a trolley on its route. Instead, there was seaweed. A school of dark minnows. A starfish on one of the pillars. Barnacles. There were supposed to be otters in the bay but he never saw them either.

The sailboats were fighting a breeze from the south. The islands were dark with firs.

When they walked past the newsstand Voyd spotted the stack of *Heralds*, the one with his new planet story. The evening edition would plant a retraction on page 17 after they found the green button. *The City Observatory apologizes for implying a new planet was discovered. This is not the case.* He felt Marjorie's hand tighten. He noticed what caught her attention just as the boy put a postcard under his shirt. Voyd also noted the silver antenna on the boy's head. A fellow Martian. Stealing? Marjorie shot him a look. The boy slipped back into the crowd.

The horror of seeing a Martian steal took them by surprise. Their far superior minds were busy looking for meaning.

Marjorie finally said, "We need to pay for that."

Voyd agreed and they started for the kiosk. Voyd thought of the destitute Martian kid driven to theft. The Martian Loyalty Oath was haunting him again. A Martian Helps Another Martian was a mantra driven into them from day one. "We'll buy a new one, but we can't let on why we're buying it. That poor kid is in enough trouble already."

They stopped in front of the postcard rack.

"Which one was it?" asked Voyd.

"Ooooof," she answered. There were a lot of them. The carrousel squeaked as it spun. "This one!"

"Al Pacino?"

She brought it to the man in the window. "How much for one of these?"

"You got a dollar?"

"Okay." She paid.

Then as they walked past the postcards, she slipped it back into the rack.

"The debt is paid," she said.

41
HELPING a FELLOW MARTIAN

Voyd linked his arm to hers. Her coat was decorated with Chronium Terns. They crossed the street and hopped a curb and stopped behind a parked truck. Glancing around, seeing they were alone, they held each other's shoulders, leaned in, and touched antennas. As they shut their eyes, a picture formed showing where the kid was.

It's not easy to find people who have this talent, it seems more like magic. A hundred million miles away, it's commonplace. All Martians have the ability.

A block from the shore, they caught up with the kid in front of the post office. Each time someone walked past, he held out his hand.

"Look at that," Voyd said. "Poor kid's begging."

"He must be shipwrecked," Marjorie said. The Chronium Terns on her coat had paled.

Voyd pulled her across the street with the crowd.

They were nearly there when the kid shocked them again. He removed his antenna, twisted the wire headband and tucked it back into his hair at a more comfortable angle. Marjorie stopped. "He's not a Martian," she breathed in relief.

"Oh no, he's seen us. He's coming this way."

The boy moved quickly across the crowded sidewalk and addressed them. "Can you help a fellow Martian down on his luck?"

"What is that? Tinfoil?" Voyd pointed at the phony antenna. "You're no Martian."

"Also, we saw you steal a postcard."

The boy looked from Marjorie to Voyd and back to her again. "I know it was wrong. I had to."

"Really?" Marjorie chimed.

"You *had* to steal a postcard?" Voyd asked, "Or what? The world would end?"

Voyd and Marjorie shot doubtful looks at each other. If they touched antennas again they would know for sure if he was lying.

The boy said, "You got a pen?"

Voyd passed him one.

The boy reached into his shirt and got the postcard. He wrote sloppy words, reading them aloud when he was done, "Dear Orphanage. This is Darro. I miss you. I was wrong to run away! I'm coming home!" The boy handed Voyd his pen and he covered his face with his sleeve. He mumbled through the cloth, "I miss them so much…"

Marjorie couldn't help it. She knew the feeling, there were loved ones on Mars she thought about every day.

With his coat sleeve still hiding him, the boy said, "I gotta go. Here. Take the card. Can you… Can you mail it for me?" He sobbed. "I'm broke!" The moment he felt Marjorie take it from him, he dropped his sleeve and ran. What were they supposed to do, chase after him? A Martian dog could do it—a Bleetnik would fly after him and round him up with ease. Then what? It was only a postcard.

"Look what he wrote," Marjorie said. She let her finger drift along the address, "The Orphanage, Dummy City, USA." Her eyes returned to Voyd's. She waited for him to say something and then he did.

"That's not a real place."

42
WALKING to SAFEWAY

Sunday morning woke Voyd and he kissed Marjorie and went to the kitchen to make Postum. He liked having a cup with her while they listened to the radio tuned to Mars. Opening the cupboard, finding an empty jar caught him by surprise. Old Mother Hubbard was no longer a rhyme. He put on a polka dotted windbreaker and set out walking to Safeway. He thought he'd get some more Clorox too. You could never have enough.

The pipe organ next door was purring. Voyd glanced at the steeple and saw the dove. Was it possible to lure it over to the other side of the duplex? He and Marjorie still didn't have a dove, let alone a pigeon…or a nice hologram garden. He remembered the paraffin flowers they grew on Mars, how pretty they were until an electric goat got them. It was easier to have holograms, they weren't real.

The store wasn't far, ten minutes each way. Some birds were awake. The neighborhood was calm enough he heard the school a block before he got there. The sound of children playing at recess. The clank of the swing chains. They ran back and forth behind the fence, going up and down slides, the monkey bars, and five of them were playing Earthlings and Martians. A girl and a boy wore paper antennas taped to their hair. A teacher on the other side of the yard blew a shrill whistle. The Earthlings chased the Martians to the jungle gym. Their game was like watching TV, outer space heroes climbing the side of a rocket, hopping through the hatch and starting the motors. Voyd hoped they would escape safely to Mars. Once in a while, he hoped he and Marjorie would too…usually after he lost another job and he was on the trolley and the Bird District was twenty minutes away, when it felt like their lives on this planet were getting nowhere.

Voyd was halfway past the school when he realized, "Wait a minute!" It's Sunday morning! There's no kids in school today! He looked closer at the playground scene. Sure enough, just around the edges, from the fence posts to the chain-link tops touched by the overhanging branches, a hologram was almost faultlessly glued. He felt like a fool falling for it. The projection box was mounted on the corner of the fence.

Up above the school, just within the square of the hologram, a flock of blue parrots flew.

43
D'S MEMORY

D is an old Martian. He used to talk about the Martian aqueducts with passion and he hoarded water jugs hidden in the nook of trees and the top shelves of fences in the leaves. He couldn't help it, his mind was going, driving him into a cloud as ghostly thick as the dust on the dead plains of the Valles Marineris Ocean. D was one of the first Martians to emigrate. He had a long white beard and wore a top hat. He still went about in his uniform overcoat. The hologram in the lining didn't work anymore, the rusted cloth was ragged and patched, the buttons were loose.

D's red pickup truck was parked at the steep top of Heron Street. He stood beside it, stirring the empty water jugs in back with a two-by-four, when Voyd said hello.

It took D a tangled moment to tear himself from whatever he was doing. His thoughts were scattered newspaper, a *Herald* that was full of out of reach stories. If he recognized Voyd, it didn't show in D's silvery eyes.

"Good morning," Voyd said.

D blinked and a memory came to him. "How's that daughter of yours?"

Voyd wasn't sure what to say.

"How old is she now?"

Voyd said a number, a year that would put a girl in preschool on Mars. It felt so real they could both picture her.

"Say, I made her something," D said.

He searched his pocket. Then he tried another pocket. His concentration was pulled thread, almost gone, when he found what he was looking for in his uniform pocket, beneath the burned-out hologram badge.

Some crows left a rooftop.

D seemed to fizzle in the dappled sunlight of the tree leaves overhead.

Voyd had to hold the Postum and Clorox tucked to one arm as he reached for D's present.

D put it on Voyd's open hand.

"Oh, look at that…" A mechanical mouse rested on Voyd's palm.

D pointed a shaky finger, a yellow fingernail close to touching, "See, you wind it up. Give it a try!" D beamed.

Voyd set his Safeway purchases down by his feet. The mouse looked like it had been in D's pocket since the war was done. It had tiny beady black eyes, and a few wrinkled whiskers stuck in a gray weather-beaten coat. An owl might have got hold of its tail. The winder key turned and tightened a spring inside that held a gear in place. The most basic contraption, stored energy, and release. Voyd spun the key five times and crouched, put the mouse on the cement and let it go. The toy ran on two small rubber wheels and chirruped like a bird. It clicked in a circle on the sidewalk concrete that was sparkling with quartz like a hundred distant stars.

44
A DAY'S TRAVEL

Meanwhile on Mars, Anthrab gathered his robe, shut his eyes, and winked from view. Martians don't need rockets or saucers or a molecular transporter. Travel to Earth is as simple as thinking it.

Not so simple for a robot though. Sophisticated as they were, they couldn't make that mental leap. If they wanted to go to a dot in the night sky, they needed a travel agent. Veda Lewismeter found one in the telephone book. It seemed reputable but you never knew. There were stories about unwary robots being hustled off to slave in the silica mines on Phobos, or worse. A robot had to be careful. Chorley's Speedy Space Service was supposed to be good, according to her friend Atharva who vacationed in Enceladus and got back in one piece.

Veda entered Chorley's tidy shop and was pleasantly surprised. She was expecting it to be like one of those film noir dives that Voyd used to watch. A bookie shop, or a pool hall, with cigarette smoke making a Frisco fog on the ceiling. Veda was impressed by the singing paraffin flowers that decorated the walls, flowing around posters of Saturn and Earth's Atlantic Ocean. There were two curtained doorways on the back wall. In front of her was Chorley—she assumed that's who it was—sitting on a stylish Medusian pommel horse. "Hello," she said.

"Yes, how may I help you? Wait!" he held her in place, "Let me guess!" He examined her Hopalong Cassidy wardrobe and the vintage sea chest beside her. "Hmmmm…Callisto?" Chorley guessed a few more times, planets, comets, even the Pleiades. Finally, she told him where and he clapped his hands, "Of course! You'll love it there! When would you like to go?"

"As soon as possible."

"As soon as possible," Chorley repeated, nodding seriously. An arm reached from the pommel holding a crystal ball for him to read. "Let's see…You're in luck! There's a supply ship leaving in ten minutes!" Hired robots had to go with the freight. The crystal ball projected pictures of her quarters. It wasn't bad. Small. A little sink, a rickety looking bed, coat hangers hooked to the wall, a porthole.

Of course any licensed travel representative was required to see a robot's paperwork and hers was in order.

"Your status says retired?" Chorley returned her permits.

"Yes, I'm going to visit my employer. He lives on Earth now."

Chorley shook his head, "A Martian living on Earth! No thanks, not for me, I wouldn't like it. It's probably different for robots though, you're adaptable, aren't you? Will you be staying the full duration?"

"Yes please."

"Okay. Two days." He stamped her passport. "Be sure you return on time." He pulled a lever and printed an orange ticket. "Just one piece of luggage?"

"Yes."

The printer started again and trundled out a baggage sticker. He took it and hopped off his pommel horse. "My! That's a long way down." He walked around her and stopped next to the sea chest and stuck the identification on: CIA-029

K48. "You're ready for Earth. Right behind the blue curtain."

She had everything she needed. Goodbye Mars. "Thank you very much."

"I hope you like it. We'll see you in two days."

After a day's travel, Voyd would get a call to pick her up.

ducks worried him

45

The NEW ATMOSPHERE

Anthrab adapted to Earth by becoming a bird. He sat on a bench. It wasn't that different than a high pommel horse. After the rush of stars and miles that melted, it took a Martian a minute or so to acclimate to the new atmosphere. To help him through that adjustment, he was singing a song. Singing calmed him, he had records on Mars he liked to play and sing along to. It didn't matter that his voice sounded to Earthlings like a Wurlitzer on a sinking ship.

Nobody was nearby, nobody alive anyway. He was in a cemetery.

When he felt better, he stood. Slowly. It felt strange wearing a suit instead of his usual robe.

He had directions. Follow the path. It took him past a pond. The ducks worried him. One of them took a step towards him. Was it growling?

He hurried. His shoes felt slippery. Getting used to his suit was going to be difficult too. Why couldn't he wear his toga? He had seen pictures of humans wearing togas in Rome, why couldn't Voyd be there? It was a mistake to send Voyd to this place to begin with. Anthrab had tried to warn Jark Narp, but his boss wouldn't listen. Anthrab's intuition was outranked.

There weren't shoes on Mars. Anthrab felt like he was running in a dream. He tried to make the shoes go faster. He looked back. The ducks weren't chasing him. The path took him safely to the street. He wished he'd done a little more research.

Anyone from a hundred million miles away who has seen the stream of American television waves passing by would think they were ready for a boulevard like this one, but Anthrab wasn't. He tried not to look like it, but he was frightened. He reminded himself his ride was arriving soon. Just be calm, he told himself…and he started singing again.

This time he was standing beside a curb on a busy street, cars rushing past, people on the sidewalk going back and forth, walking past him staring holding their ears. A policeman watching traffic heard him too and winced. A leashed dog barked at the shrill scrawl.

46
TURNING in TIME

Voyd got home with Postum, Clorox, and a mouse in his coat. Marjorie was listening to folksongs on Mars Radio. He put his purchases on the table and embraced her. With a voice like Valentino, he told her, "I've travelled across the universe to find you!"

In their embrace, her voice muffled, "The vacuum cleaner broke again."

"Oh no! I just fixed that!"

Marjorie rolled her eyes. She had seen him fixing it last week with duct tape and a paperclip.

He could see the machine standing by the window where Joan Crawford used to be.

"What's wrong with it?"

Marjorie told him it wasn't blowing out dust—unlike their Earth counterparts, Martian vacuum cleaners are filled with particles of dust from their planet and when they're working they make the finest layer across the floor and furniture.

Voyd crouched next to the machine and looked at it and it didn't take him long to conclude all the tin bits and duct tape had reached their limit. If it wasn't blowing out a settling cloud, what was the point?

"Let's have a cup of Postum and decide what to do."

Voyd let the vacuum rock back to its upright position, stork-like and silent.

Their kitchen was warm, the radio was on. Mars Variety Hour. She had a telephone book open on the counter. She was already searching, a pen, a scrap of paper, some numbers written down. "You remember when Bernard told us he was done with the wax museum? He said he was going to work at his brother's vacuum cleaner shop."

"That's right," Voyd said. He turned the phone book around so he could read it.

Marjorie said, "Didn't Bernard say Better Vacuums was their shop?"

"Hmmm…There's also a Best Vacuums listed. That might be better."

"Better than Better?"

"Isn't Best better?"

"Nothing is better than better," Marjorie said confidently. "Better is always better."

Martians didn't have this trouble with their words.

The water in the kettle was boiling. On Mars the water had to travel thousands of miles in canals and aqueducts. Here, you could stand in the rain and fill a cup for Postum. If it wasn't raining, you could turn a tap and the water would flow and flow, enough to fill a pond, a lake, an ocean. She fixed two cups and stirred them with a chirping spoon.

Voyd looked at the spot where their wax guests spent the night "Do you miss Joan and Twisty?"

She set their cups on the table and sat down with him. "Yeah, I do a little. Maybe we could find some plants to replace them. A snapdragon and a foxglove."

He wrapped his hands around his cup. "Should we stop by the zoo on the way home and check on them?"

Marjorie sighed, "What are we going to do with them?"

"I don't know. Keep an eye on them, make sure they're okay. They must be important if MarsCorp went to all this trouble to raid The House of Stars and rip up every wax figure in town. Those two might be the only survivors. Such as they are."

Funny, Marjorie and Voyd wouldn't be going back. Things would happen and it wouldn't matter. That wax ball of Joan and Twisty would remain in the hollow tree, turning in time into the largest honey beehive in Woodland Park.

47
BETTER VACUUMS

They found parking under the tall monorail track, right in front of Better Vacuums. It reminded Voyd of parking scooters under the aqueduct pylons back home, when they used to climb the ivy to the top and sit with their feet in the rusted water trickle. Marjorie squeezed his hand—she had been thinking the same thing. Thoughts like that are instant telepathy. But that was ages ago and this was them now, on Earth, carrying a broken vacuum cleaner.

"There he is, I see him." With her hand held low to her hip, Marjorie twitched a pointing finger.

Voyd looked at the big window and saw Bernard in a crowd of vacuums. Voyd wondered if he said goodnight to each and every one of them as he did at the wax museum

"That's him alright." Just before he opened the door, Voyd said, "I wonder if he misses the wax museum." As soon as he followed Marjorie in, he thought, probably not, this place was just another sort of museum. A string of bells clattered on the doorframe as he shut the door.

Bernard was holding a bellows. He looked over a worktable piled high with parts and he recognized his customers. "Good morning!"

The front of the store was a showroom and the back was where repairs were done.

Marjorie and Voyd drifted towards him, eyes going here and there, distracted by the attractions. Marjorie stopped at a display of air-actuated vibrating reeds encased on the wall. A button activated each of them and hummed a different frequency.

"What's that you've got with you?" Bernard asked.

"Our vacuum cleaner isn't working right. I did everything I could for it. I've been tinkering with it since we got it. I think we need a professional opinion." Voyd placed the vacuum on a cleared section of the table. "By the way, how are you doing here?"

"It's lovely. Everything is made to last. I don't miss the museum at all." He swiveled on his chair to find some tools.

"See if they're hiring." Marjorie whispered in Voyd's ear.

Voyd sighed and he asked.

"Can you fix vacuums?" Bernard replied.

Voyd said, "Sure."

"Maybe it will be steady work?" Marjorie whispered. "That would be nice."

It was something for him to think about. He liked the shop.

Bernard swiveled back. "Let's see what you've got." He turned the vacuum cleaner and unsnapped the panel. "Spinet, reed hook, flanges, valve springs, pallet rods, sharps, punchings, suction pistons, tunings...Here's your problem... You just need to turn this to the right setting. It's set on suction." He twisted the dial. He gave Voyd a hard look, "Maybe you don't know so much about vacuum cleaners."

No, I guess I don't, Voyd realized.

Bernard replaced the panel. "But I can promise you, this one won't last. The parts are worn through. All this tape and jerry-rigging won't help anymore. You need a new one."

"A new one?"

Voyd gaped with such obvious horror Bernard laughed. Those pinchpenny Martians! "Don't worry. We have a nice selection of reconditioned merchandise especially built for Martian needs. I'll even give you a deal on a bagful of dust."

48
The HOOVER CONSTELLATION

In the end they bought a rebuilt Hoover Constellation. "Still the best vacuum," Bernard told them. And he made a point of twice showing Voyd the silver toggle switch for suction. Marjorie opened the car door and Voyd seated their purchase. The shape was a little like Joan Crawford after she melted. Above them the monorail track whined with the approach of a train. Pigeons scattered for somewhere else.

Voyd started the car and could see the rushing reflection from above checkering the hood of their car. "You sure you don't want to go to the zoo? We're not far."

She tilted a look at him and said, "I'm going to put *you* in the zoo."

He laughed. She could be Audrey Meadows. He steered away from the curb and sped around a rikshaw and a five-wheeled tricycle hauling newsprint. The zoo did have a Martian exhibit. Voyd pictured himself sitting on a zompf reading the *Herald*, doing a crossword while fieldtrips went by the glass.

"That was nice of Bernard to include the Martian dust. That doesn't come cheap."

Voyd nodded, "He probably has a dealer. I hope it isn't that guy with the quality used bacon." They both made a face. "Some of these guys will trick you into buying dust from Earth. Sand cut with paprika. We've been lucky so far."

"Bernard wouldn't do that, would he?"

"No, I don't think so. He doesn't seem like the shady sort. We'll find out, I guess."

"Look at the animals!" Marjorie pointed at a row of eight ducks on the sidewalk. People made way for them as the mother and babies waddled through. Marjorie was smiling. Being from Mars, she was constantly surprised by the new things around her.

"And what's that?" Voyd stared at the field passing on the left side of the car. "What's a field doing in the middle of the city? With a cow!" He slowed the car and drove off the paving and parked.

"What are you doing?"

"Hang on. I'll be right back." He jumped from the car.

The car tires were resting on green topsoil. Specks of buttercups and burdock grew. Voyd climbed the cedar post fence and hopped onto the grass on the other side. The ground had a little give to it, like pressing a loaf of pumpernickel between your hands. The black and white cow grazed off in the tenement shadows.

Voyd was done in a minute, jumping behind the wheel holding a bunch of flowers for Marjorie. "Daisies. Your favorite. They're growing wild in there."

Marjorie held them until they got home to Warbler Street and she set them next to the sink. While Voyd carried the vacuum into their living room and untangled the extension wire, she poured water into a vase. As soon as the stems touched tap water, they popped in her hands, changing into wheaty brush weeds and a sprig of dried coriander. "Voyd!"

"Flimnap!" A curse in the other room.

"Voyd, can you come to the kitchen?"

He garbled something again. A chair fell over.

She held the handful of rubble-grown weeds which must have been hexed with a hologram and she was about to say something about it when Voyd appeared in the doorframe, covered in an orange burst of cardamom dust that went off like a timebomb when he plugged in their new Constellation.

They both got stuck with holograms.

Instead of a reconditioned 1957 Hoover, Voyd held a plastic broom.

49
TOKYO PIANO

"Good morning. I hope this phone call finds you well. I am calling to introduce our company, Tokyo Piano, specializing in piano manufacturing and international trade for over eighty years. With a commitment to creating a favorable business environment, we have established a high-quality piano manufacturing base catering to people from all walks of life. Our pianos are more than product, they are renowned for their exceptional craftsmanship and precision. We are confident that our mutual collaboration will bring success and growth to both of us." Voyd paused to catch his breath. What a script! And he actually got to the end of it!—usually they hung up on him. Some of these old people seemed so alone they would listen as if he was Guy Lombardo on the radio. But everyone had their limit. A piano wouldn't fit in a pensioner's cell. "Okay..." he replied. "That's okay, we can manufacture pianos of various specifications and export them in the way you like…Okay, okay, I understand, thank you. I certainly appreciated our talk." Voyd put the phone back into its cradle. It was like fishing: sooner or later he'd get a bite. He checked a box and wrote a brief comment. He glanced at the clock, returned to the phone and picked it up for his next call.

The Labor Now calendar tacked to the cubicle wall was a photograph of Fiji.

"Hello, I'm looking forward to discussing potential business opportunities with—" That's all he got to say. That's how it usually went.

That call was over quickly. He clocked it in and dialed a new number. Voyd took a deep breath and tried again, "Good morning. My name is Voyd and I am Martian. I have been engaged in piano manufacturing and international trade for thirty years and have rich experience in piano manufacturing. We would like to introduce our company, Tokyo Piano, and our exceptional products. Our pianos boast outstanding craftsmanship, durability and offer a comfortable playing experience. Notably, our pianos are equipped with high-quality components sourced from Japan and Germany. Moreover, our competitive pricing makes them even more attractive. Additionally, all our pianos come with a correction-unit so anyone can play like Mozart or Fats Waller. We also provide lifetime after-sales service. Considering all these features, are you astonished to find that our pianos are priced so reasonably as well? Isn't it an enticing offer? Isn't it a valuable investment? Isn't it a business opportunity worth pursuing? Isn't it—Hello? Are you still there?" Isn't it something when the sound of your voice goes over a canyon wall and never comes back as an echo? Voyd wrote the details. Things weren't going so well.

Just then the phone rang. Was it supposed to do that? Was Labor Now testing him? Was some other seller hustling him? Voyd was a little afraid to answer it. After the fourth ring though, he gave in. "Hello, Tokyo Piano…"

Marjorie laughed. "Hi Tokyo Piano, it's your wife."

"Oh hi! What a relief to hear your voice!" It really was. "Is everything okay?" Nobody climbing in windows, nothing melting?

"Veda just called me. She's here on Earth. At the rocketport! She wants you to give her a ride to our house."

50
STARLINGS

Veda Lewismeter waited for Voyd at the Martian rocketport outside of town off the Pacific Highway. She sat on a cardboard box with her feet resting on the sea chest. The box of sandfruit had been her chair for a day of interplanetary travel. The rocket cargo hold around her had been filled with more boxes and pallets piled high with bags of Martian dust. It wasn't exactly comfortable, the pictures they showed her at the travel agency bore no similarity. No sink, no bed. There was no porthole. The only light came from a lantern on a hook by the hatch.

Her book crackled. She turned another mica page. A silvery reflection hovered on her tan waistcoat.

She wasn't the only robot in the room. Thirty feet from her, a shoeshiner stood next to his stand. He tried his best with her and got nowhere. He was quiet, almost sulking, until the door opened and Voyd walked in. The robot barked, "Shine, mister?"

Voyd had his eyes fixed on Veda. He waved off the intrusive robot.

"Veda!" he blurted. "What are you doing here?"

"Rude," she huffed. She shut her book and stood up. She avoided answering that question until they were in the car. That's when she told him, "I'm done with Mars."

"What? Didn't I retire you? Weren't you going to spend the rest of your days on the beaches of Ganymede?"

"I'm not going back. I want a different planet. This one."

"You're moving here?"

"Why not? It is very pleasant and not expensive."

"You can't! Robots are prohibited from staying on Earth for more than two days!"

"Rules are made to be broken."

"Wow," Voyd said. "What are you going to do? How can you survive?"

"I heard that Labor Now is a good place to start."

"Where will you stay? Where am I taking you?"

"Where I've always belonged. With you and the missus. I'm sure you still observe the Martian Oath and will welcome a fellow needy Martian. Look at that! What is that?"

Voyd looked out her window and managed to answer, "That's a blue jay. It's a bird."

"Look at it go!" she cried. Martians are fascinated by birds. Voyd and Marjorie liked to pull up chairs to the window and watch the starlings decorate the telephone line. They could watch for hours.

51
TORCHY BLANE

Another thing Veda noticed was the wax figures. Here and there, it was as if some noticeable percent of the town's population had turned to wax. A cyclone had snatched up certain luminaries and cast them aside. Cab Calloway on a fire escape. Rags Ragland from the chest up, stuck to the top of a blue letter box on the corner, watching traffic like the Cheshire Cat.

Veda told him the latest from Mars and Voyd caught her up on everything that happened since the wax museum melted. That event had changed all their lives. He felt too ashamed to tell her what he spent on a vacuum cleaner that turned out to be a broom. She would be appalled, back home she took care of all their needs.

"Over there is the Safeway, where we shop for food."

"Shop?"

"This isn't Mars. We have to *buy* our food. And everything else. Everything's for sale."

"Right." She watched the people bringing grocery bags to their cars. A seagull pounced on a crust of bread. "I don't know how you can get used to it."

"Labor Now is supposed to acclimate me. But I'm still surprised." He also felt he was getting used to a state of surprise. "We live in the Bird District, the Bird Streets. If you ever get lost, you need to know that. We're almost to our street. Warbler. See the sign names on the corner?"

Veda couldn't hide her reaction as the car turned on Warbler and all the holograms greeted her. To see this many all at once was astounding—Martians didn't need holograms anymore, they were considered a little…misguided. But that didn't stop MarsCorp from realizing their potential for the conquest of Earth. "Which one is yours?" she asked, expecting a Buckminster Fuller geodesic sphere.

"The apartment by the blue cathedral." Among the Earthlings, Marjorie and Voyd felt compelled to cloak their duplex in a mirage. They wanted to fit in.

"Oh yes!" she grinned. "It looks like Torchy Blane could live there."

"That's possible. Maybe you can be her. My neighbor needs another dove for his steeple, don't you think?"

"What about on this side of your house? Is that a ranch? Is that a cowboy riding a horse?"

"That's Oatmeal."

As their car drifted into the curb and parked, Oatmeal Houston reined his horse over closer to the hologram line, careful not to cross it. He waited until Veda left the car then he tipped his ten-gallon hat, "Howdy, ma'am."

"Oh, hello."

He admired her Hopalong Cassidy attire and told her so. Why, the bluebonnets out back in the pasture couldn't hold a candle to her, he said.

Voyd hated to interrupt their wooing, but he was carrying a heavy sea chest and he needed her to get the door.

52
The SOUND of the RAIN

What did Marjorie think of having Veda back in their house? She missed the robot. Someone to do the errands while they were gone, someone to make something other than Martian Dollar food—no offence—to come home to good meals and clean rooms, having someone to keep them company with Martian memories and someone who would sit with them at nightfall and watch old movies, or play harp. At the end of their day, Veda had the corner where Joan Crawford used to be.

On rainy nights, Martians had trouble sleeping. Voyd rolled away from Marjorie and got out of bed. Some warm Postum might help. He walked through the dark room and hall to the kitchen. The cupboard squeaked as it opened. He got a jar, set it on the counter, got two cups and a spoon. He knew Marjorie would be staring at the ceiling wondering what he was doing. Once she heard the water pouring in the kettle, she would know.

That's when he heard the sound of the rain. He walked around the counter towards the living room and he could feel the prickling weather on his skin. "Veda?" Her silhouette stood against the blue open window, admiring Warbler Street. The neon fuzz of the casino marquee across the street shined the rivet droplets of rain drifting into the room. The long curtains waved.

An orange sticker glowed CIA-029 K48 like jack-o-lantern eyes on the sea chest by Veda's chair. He heard her breathe in deeply. Why? She didn't need oxygen, she had another need for molecules, they stirred memory. Martian robots could remember millions of years. Once there were oceans on their planet and night rains like this reminded her.

"Mmmmmm," Veda said, "Earth. It wanted me here. A robot gets used to following signals. I went to the travel agency. I got a ticket. There were two doors. I chose the one for Earth. Do you mind the window open?"

"No, I like this weather too. Sometimes it rains and I stand in it and it feels like I could be washed out to sea, other times it's like this, and I get hypnotized by it like a Berva cat."

"Someone on Mars gave me a present for you. I don't know who they were, they didn't say, must have been someone you knew." She turned to the sea chest. The orange letters and numbers glowed on her legs. She opened the lid. "Oh by the way…" she moved a sweater aside and got a stack of Martian junkmail and bills. "These were supposed to be paid before you and the missus left."

"What? Those are all overdue?"

She shook her head. How unlike a robot not to care. "I couldn't have afforded the fare to Earth if I paid those."

"Don't you think they'll come looking for me?"

"All the way from Mars? Ahah, here it is." She held out a Martian radio. A beauty. He had seen it in the Martian catalog that came in the mail. Apparently someone knew they needed it—their other radio had long rabbit ears with tinfoil ball tips, and when it couldn't quite catch the distant electromagnetic waves of the red planet, it fizzled and squelched.

Voyd tossed the envelopes to the side so he could cup his hands around their new radio.

waves of the red planet

53
OTHER MESSAGES

If he had been attentive, Voyd would have recalled all the times he saw CIA-029 K48. At the bookstore, graffiti on the street, a license plate, and now it was glowing on Veda's luggage. Another time, when he got a sandwich at the automat, instead of cheese there was a piece of yellow paper. CIA-029 K48 was written on it. He looked at the wall formed of little glass doors leading to the kitchen, the cooks, the bustling staff, then he crumpled the paper and left it on the tray by his plate. One day at Shell's Diner, he put a dime in the jukebox. CIA-029 K48 was carved next to the label in the Lena Horne shellac. And then there was CIA-029 K48 written on the breath of the morning trolley window. Voyd wiped the steam away so he could see where he was going. By now it should have been familiar—CIA-029 K48 was everywhere—but he must have thought nothing of it, it must have been like all the other messages jangling for attention. He turned off the stove light and went back to the bedroom with two cups of Postum in the dark.

Another Martian on that rainy night was also restless. Anthrab didn't look quite comfortable in his business suit. He missed his shiny tin mortar hat and robe. While the rain slicked around his glass walls, he was crumpled in a phonebooth, holding for the operator to connect him with Mars. Funny, even though it was raining, above the 7-Eleven parking lot, bats were flapping around the lit-up sign. The world couldn't stop on account of a little rain. Moths had to leave their wool and perish in the bright light.

"Yes, hello," Anthrab said. "Hello sir." His reflection grinned back at him, foolish beneath a white fedora. "It's raining here, sir. Can you believe it? Would you like to hear it?" He was going to hold the receiver outside the narrow doorway, but Jark Narp's voice barked in his ear. "Yes sir," Anthrab said. "No, you don't have to...No sir, I won't talk about the weather anymore...I understand that, sir...No, I haven't seen Voyd yet. I had a little trouble with the authorities. Did you know I got ticketed by the police when I got here? They said I was disturbing the peace…Yes, sir…Yes, I was singing…I know it's a bad habit, sir. In the future I intend to be more careful."

While he talked, he kept an eye on the bats. They flitted in orbit round and round. Somehow it didn't seem real. He supposed they could be holograms. He could check an invoice directory at the factory tomorrow and see if 7-Eleven ordered them. It looked like Martian work. He was just curious, that's all.

When the call from Earth was over, he hung up the phone and went out to the street where his gondola hologram waited for him at the curb.

54
A RETURN ROCKET at DAWN

Sunlight pleated in the curtains. Voyd hid beside them and watched the two Martians continue down the path and out of the hologram, onto the sidewalk to their parked velocipede. He took a deep breath of relief and turned. Veda and Marjorie watched him from the kitchen.

"Are they gone?"

Voyd exhaled. "Yes. That was a close one. I thought they were after me…for all those unpaid bills."

"Why do they want Veda?" Marjorie asked. "She's our robot, she's allowed to be with us if she wants."

"Not exactly," said Voyd.

Veda explained, "I only got a two-day pass to Earth. I was supposed to be on a return rocket at dawn today."

Marjorie looked confused. "Well, we can extend

your stay, can't we?"

"Two days is the maximum robots are allowed. It's the law." Veda glanced at the silver watch on her wrist, "As of two hours ago, I'm considered AWOL."

"They're giving us an hour to get to the rocketport," Voyd said. "You better pack."

"Oh please! I don't want to go back to Mars, I want to stay! I want to be here with you on this charming planet."

Marjorie put a comforting hand on the robot's shoulder.

"It's not fair! They don't give me time to do anything! I just got here and I'm already leaving?" Veda covered her eyes and sobbed.

Marjorie looked at Voyd, "Isn't there a way we—?"

"No. It's out of the question, dear. We can't have a renegade robot in our house. It's bad enough I'm wanted for outstanding debt, we're not going to—"

"Oatmeal!" Veda exclaimed.

"What?"

"Oatmeal Houston," she gushed.

"What about him?"

"He serenaded me at the window last night. After you were gone. He stood on the other side of his fence in the moonlight and played me a song on his guitar. Oh, Oatmeal will save me!"

"You're kidding."

Marjorie's eyes flashed, "Let's ask him! Maybe Veda can stay on his ranch for a while. Just until things blow over." Before Voyd could reply or otherwise opinionate, they whisked past him, leaving the door open on their way out.

55
The MULTIPLE DIMENSIONS of REINCARNATION

Oatmeal Houston stopped cutting brush when he saw Veda. He wiped a plaid shirt sleeve across his brow and approached the fence in slow but steady strides. Lyrical as Smith Ballew he removed his tall hat and smiled good morning.

Voyd decided he had no choice but to join them. By clicking a button, his robe became a rustic Italian peasant's wear.

"It's a mighty fine day," Oatmeal was saying. Warbler Street was still waking, the people in hologram houses were on their way to work. He had taken a shine to her. He waited all night until morning to see her.

"Not so fine for me," Veda replied. "I'm a wanted fugitive. I don't know what I'll do."

That's when Voyd arrived behind his wife, while Veda spelled out her predicament.

"Don't you worry," the cowboy consoled her. It was his solemn duty, he promised, to look out for her, to make sure she was always safe. He invited her to come through the gate, "You don't have to go to Mars. You can join me in the wide prairies where nobody will find us."

Veda admired the territory, the sunlit sage, and the hills rolling towards ragged mountains. "It really is beautiful. Almost like Mars."

"That's true," said Marjorie. She had never seen the lot without a hologram. For all she knew, a ranch really did carve its way beyond the city to a horizon no one could doubt. She never went to the window between 2:30 and 3 AM, long enough to see that blink of reality. What you don't know can't hurt you is what an Earthling would say. Those two Martians in their velocipede could return any moment. If Veda could hide in a hologram for a while that seemed as good a solution as stuffing Joan Crawford and Conway Twitty inside a hollow tree.

The decision wasn't difficult for Veda, she needed an escape. "Okay," she said. "I'll go."

"That's fine!" Oatmeal beamed. "You've made me so happy!" He gave a whistle and two horses came from the shade of a sycamore.

"Oh look!" Veda cried. "Cows!"

"Horses, ma'am," said Oatmeal. "One for you and one for me."

He unlooped the gate lariat, "Right this way," and she sunk into the mirage. Veda didn't need to change—in her Hopalong Cassidy threads she already belonged to the Wild West.

Voyd squinted at what might be a distant buffalo.

Oatmeal and Veda rode the horses towards that same distance.

Who really knew what Veda was seeing, once you broke into the hologram, everything changed for you. Places and faces, anything could be, and anyone could be awaiting her like the multiple dimensions of reincarnation. And if she turned around, what would she see of the world she left? The world she lived in was the world of dreams.

Marjorie said, "Don't worry, she can take care of herself, she always has."

Voyd held his hand over the fence, dipping into the hologram to pick a yellow rose for Marjorie. As the stem bent through the barrier, it became a carnation stalk from the Safeway dollar rack. He let go of it and stood up. The horses were gone when Voyd looked for them again.

"They're gone," Marjorie said. She squeezed his arm, "Postum?"

"That would be nice."

From down Warbler Street in the other direction came the rattly sound of a Martian velocipede nearing.

56
The SONG in the AIR

"It's time," Anthrab told him, "We're going to give you your last job."

Voyd was still getting over the shock of not being arrested by Martian debt collectors.

Anthrab continued, "We feel you'd do better at the factory with us. Maybe pushing broom at first, but at least you won't make any more trouble."

Marjorie slipped her arm around her husband.

"You too, Marjorie. We've been most impressed with your steady hard work and loyalty. We have a place for you at MarsCorp."

Voyd asked, "What about my unpaid bills from Mars? I—"

"Don't worry about them, Mr. Lewismeter. We've been garnishing your wages and will continue to until they're paid off."

Voyd slumped as the great weight of that was removed.

"That's your house, eh? I bet you'll be glad to come live with us in MartianTown, won't you?"

Marjorie clapped a hand to her mouth. She nearly cried with relief. There were things about that duplex no hologram could hide.

"By the way, is it true you had some museum displays in there?"

"Yes," Voyd caught himself quickly, "No. I mean we did. We only stored them overnight for an Earthling, but we brought them back to his museum, to the alley, and dumped them. I don't know what happened to them after that."

"Hmmm." Anthrab let that answer stick to the air. "Anyway, I'm here to take you both to MarsCorp, to show you what you've been working for." The back door of the velocipede responded with a click and opened.

"What—right now?" Voyd glanced at his rustic Italian peasant wardrobe, his doublet, his breeches, his duckbill shoes, and he knew they wouldn't do. With a simple click, his green suit reappeared, complete with brown fedora. Marjorie too chose something more formal. Neither one had been to MarsCorp yet, they had been striving all this time to get there.

The three of them settled on the fine Corinthian leather backseat of the velocipede. Anthrab told the driver to proceed, and the Bird District passed them by in the opera windows. The 8-Track played softly, the traffic got heavier as they rolled along the boulevard, and soon they were caught in a snarl of morning rush-hour.

Such an uncivilized way to go about your morning, Anthrab thought, like ants toiling in a line, what a way to relate to your planet. Not one of them stopped to climb a lamppost, to sit up there in the morning sun. The birds would— they would sing all day, on the sidewalks, gutters, electricity wires—once Mars had its way, the birds would be the song in the air. Stuck in a rumble of traffic and lost in thought, Anthrab began to hum.

57
The SWEEPER

MarsCorp was located atop Jupiter Hill among the trees and disintegrating late morning fog. There was no need for hologram projection, the building was made of genuine marble and steel and twinkling glass. The velocipede slipped past one guard booth and then another before they stopped at a smooth arched sandstone entrance. Anthrab welcomed them and led them inside the factory. The burnished floors shined like the fabled plains of Acidalia. They stepped over a narrow creek of running water on their way to the camphor trees twined around the elevator doors.

Before they reached the far wall, Anthrab steered their attention towards a custodian running a sweeper machine, sowing a thin film of dust on the floor. "Soyb!"

The driver recognized who was calling his name and raised a hand in recognition. His arm was thin as rolled newspaper. The sweeper rocked and veered slightly and Soyb dropped his hand back to the controls to wrestle the engine.

Anthrab urged him to continue with his work, apologized and gave the sweeper room to clear. "That's Soyb for you. He's quite a character." When they reached the elevator he told Voyd, "I've heard that Mr. Narp has Soyb in mind as your mentor."

They got into the elevator and spread out a little. This was their invitation to MarsCorp and could be their big chance at calling this place home, but Voyd wasn't sure he wanted to drive a sweeper down every day. Voyd saw Marjorie look at him and he looked away. Anthrab was staring straight ahead at the crack between the elevator doors where the light flashed as the floors went down.

"What about me?" Marjorie asked Anthrab. "Is there a job for me?"

"Oh sure. We're going to it."

She looked up at the floor number panel. The numbers were dropping.

Being from Mars they were used to living in tunnels to avoid meteorites and alpha rays. On

Earth they didn't need to, but old habits die hard. They were used to being underground. Another half a minute and they slowed to a stop at the basement.

Their perception of MarsCorp changed the second the doors unsealed.

The elevator doors opened and Voyd felt like he was right back at prison when he was Don Knotts.

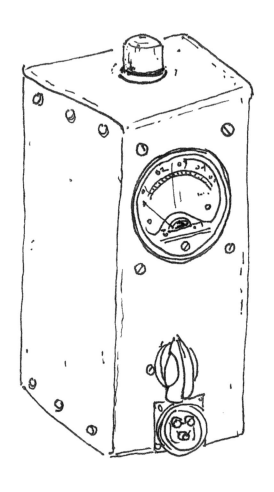

snapped into view

58
The MORNING HERALD

"We need the hologram turned back on!" Anthrab barked.

Marjorie and Voyd stared at the scene unfolded on the factory floor, the real MarsCorp.

Anthrab didn't bother sending them back on the elevator, he was too panicked. The jobs on Mars weren't like this. When he worked for Mr. Narp the most he had to do was run a report on mica. "What fuse box?" he crabbed. "Where is it?" This was not the same placid Martian who sat in a luxury velocipede this morning.

It took another long minute for the hologram to restart. A wildflower prairie on Mars snapped into view, flowers served by bees and other flying bugs, hummingbirds, ladybugs.

Anthrab was still out of breath. "I don't want you to jump to any conclusions about the work here."

The bright field was almost blinding so fierce was its cheery determination to glow.

Marjorie turned to Anthrab, "What is it I was supposed to do?"

"There's a dial. Over—other there, by the waterfall. We need someone to record and manage the uh, output levels. Mistakes won't happen that way."

They stared at Anthrab the way people watched The Flying Wallendas fall.

Anthrab tried to place his words carefully, "You're concerned. I can tell. A little horrified? You probably aren't quite as keen to work here, I understand that, but you know our mission here on Earth."

They knew alright, in theory, but there was nothing like seeing it right before your eyes.

"Can we go back now?" Marjorie said. "I have a shift at the Nimbus."

"Me too," said Voyd. "At Labor Now."

A postcard was placed in the air, but it wasn't fooling anyone. Anthrab was worried. This wasn't the way it was supposed to go. No Martian ever refused MarsCorp. What would Jark Narp say?

Voyd took Marjorie's hand and startled as

suddenly his green suit turned back into a maroon bathrobe. That was the problem with the dollar store holograms, they couldn't be counted on. Inferior holograms only held for a while. Like the humans, he had to buy them by the handful to keep his shape. The one on his robe lining was reliable for around the house, if he didn't want to get dressed just to go out on their path to retrieve the morning *Herald*.

59
MARTIAN RADIO

It was a tense ride from Jupiter Hill to the Bird District. Anthrab hummed the entire way. Marjorie nudged Voyd and pointed at the robot. There it was, moving glacially slow, away from the water in their direction. When they got out of the velocipede, neither Voyd or Marjorie could say anything, not until they were in their own hologram holding cups of Postum.

"I'm going to work, Voyd. I don't ever want to go back to MarsCorp."

By now, Voyd was in his real green suit. He also had their new Martian radio. He set it on the tabletop and sat down with his cup. When he turned the power switch, the radio said one thing, "CIA-029 K48," over and over.

"What is that?"

"I'm not sure." He turned it off and put it down.

Marjorie finished her Postum and put the cup in the sink. "I have to get ready."

He supposed he did too. At least he could check in. The air would do him good, he could ride his bike, the long way that went under the elevated monorail. He took his cup to the sink and put it by hers. Marjorie needed the same relief, to roll down the windows and drive. They wanted to forget what they had seen at MarsCorp.

"CIA-029 K48." The radio brought itself to life. "CIA-029 K48."

This time when Voyd picked up the radio, he examined it long enough to find the settings on the back, the small dials with letters and numbers. It continued to chant, "CIA-029 K48."

Marjorie was coming down the stairs, "It sounds like a code." she called.

"Or a channel, the frequency for a radio station maybe." He started to move the dials, "C…I…A…-…Zero…Two…"

For once Marjorie didn't mention one of those old Earth movies Voyd liked, where Victor Sen Yung would be doing this very same thing in a murky black and white set.

"Four…Eight," Voyd finished.

The radio hiccupped CIA-029 K48 one last time then announced, "Finally! What took you so long?"

"Who is this?"

Marjorie came next to Voyd, wrapping a shawl around herself. "What's going on?"

"I'm talking to someone on the radio."

The radio said, "Is that you, Marjorie?"

She pulled back a little. "Yes..."

"What a relief! I think we'll have better luck getting through to you."

Voyd looked at his wife. She looked at the radio.

"We're listening," Marjorie told it. They were both staring at the radio broadcasting with the intensity of *Blackstone the Magic Detective*.

In a voice all the way from Mars, it spoke: "It's about the robot."

60
LOOK OUT ANY WINDOW

"Robot?"

The radio answered Marjorie, "The one Voyd started. The hundred foot one. Look out any window. You can't miss it."

"We know it," Voyd said, "What about it?"

Marjorie gave him a squeeze and a quick look. There was no point getting angry with a radio.

"It's no mystery," the radio continued, "We were hoping Voyd could figure it out on his own—I don't know how many clues we gave him—but apparently not enough. I wish we would have tried with you, Marjorie. You knew right away it's a code."

Voyd was about to say something.

"But Voyd is to be commended for knowing enough to save Joan Crawford. She is an essential part of our plan."

Voyd recalled with dismay that Joan was no

205

more than a big ball of wax now. Could she even be recognized in a Hollywood lineup?

"What exactly is your plan?" Marjorie said.

The radio introduced itself, the voice belonged to the Martian underground. Not all Martians wanted the conquest of Earth, that was no way to visit a planet. "You both have spent plenty of time with humans. You don't seem to have been made bitter following the lives they lead." No, Marjorie told the radio, she and her husband may have grown closer to them, especially after what they had seen at MarsCorp and the radio crowed, "Exactly! MarsCorp is only steps away from Earth's domination. Once they get people trapped in holograms, it's all over, the invasion is over."

Marjorie sat down at the kitchen table. Her waitressing receipt notepad fell from her apron pocket and she picked it up. Voyd stared at the window. Around the cedar branches he could see a prairie shimmer. "So, you need our help," Marjorie said.

"With the robot?" Voyd added.

"When it gets here, all you have to do is enter the code."

Marjorie's eyes widened, "It's coming here?"

"It's on its way."

"Then what happens if we enter the code?"

"No more holograms," the radio said.

Voyd laughed, he couldn't help it. Nerves.

"It won't get here until late evening."

Marjorie said, "That's hours from now." She stood up, "And I'm due at work."

The radio was surprised, "You're going off to serve tables knowing what you now know?" It whistled. "I guess that's commendable."

"Me too," said Voyd. His bicycle was leaned in the backyard, tied to the handrail like a horse.

61
PHEASANT STREET

Voyd got pretty close to the giant robot when he reached Aurora. Apparently it was preparing to stride over that busy avenue, balancing on one leg, the other lifted high in the air, coming down nearly imperceptibly. You could hear it, above the sound of tires and carriages, a slight almost wooden creak in the air.

Voyd didn't bother with his bicycle hologram. So what if his Schwinn wasn't him driving a new Ford Millipede? At the crumbling end of a 7-Eleven parking lot, he put the kickstand down and sat watching the robot. The sun glared on it, shadowing the dents and scratches. The robot had been trespassing over the city with no discernible destination until now. It was pointed for a duplex on Warbler Street.

A man came out of 7-Eleven, pressed a button on his dollar hologram and turned into Derry, the trolley entertainer. Voyd's immediate reaction was to flee. He turned the handlebars and jumped on the pedals. The tire spokes began to blur. He was afraid to turn around and see that red devil suit chasing him. Away was all that mattered.

That's how he found himself on a random Bird Street, not one he'd been to before, Pheasant Street. Before the Martians arrived, it was a gently sloping hill with small houses with small front yards facing the road. Telephone poles wired the houses together, strung them like dull fish caught from a pond. You could live on that street and never really be able to describe it. Tired, Voyd dismounted and pushed his bike up the sloping sidewalk. He could tell by the holograms what the people here had been dreaming of all along.

Pretty soon it would all change back to what it was. The Martian radio told Voyd and Marjorie, "We had to be clever. MarsCorp is onto our plans, only partly though. They raided the museum, they know we're using a wax museum figure with a relay unit in it. They're looking for Joan Crawford, but they don't know that she and the robot are connected. They need each other to work. You enter the code, the robot tells her, she relays the message and that's it. No more holograms."

A week ago, would Voyd have considered this? All it took was a visit to the MarsCorp basement to change his mind.

There was a ragged engine noise coming, an old Econoline climbing Pheasant Street. The windshield was too bright with sunshine reflection to tell who was driving. Voyd thought it might be Laurel and Hardy again and he raised a hand to it as it passed. They must not have recognized him, not being Don Knotts anymore.

a ragged engine noise

62
The RED PLANET WAVELENGTH

Marjorie could see all of town from the Nimbus. The candles were lit on the tables, it was the quiet time after lunch, before the dinner crowd. She stood at the window until she spotted the robot frozen halfway across Aurora Avenue causing traffic to stall and dam up around his big metal foot. She took a sip of Postum. The robot would reach their house tonight and tomorrow would be a different world. No more holograms…She touched her hand to her hair and brushed across her antenna. That sent a signal to Voyd, to know she was thinking of him. She hoped Labor Now had something good for him. He would feel a little bee of electricity from her.

He didn't. Voyd didn't go to Labor Now. His antenna wasn't on. He was watching a movie at the Avalon.

Her next message said: Whatever happens, we're together.

That didn't reach him either.

A telegram would have found him, delivered down the aisle by an usher with a flashlight, calling his name.

A cloud drifted across the window. It never occurred to her before that maybe the clouds begin at the Nimbus, maybe the cook was in the kitchen stirring a big pot of them, escorting them out the window, pushing them like sheep into the sky. A spice rack over the stove held rain, snow, hail, and rainbow.

"Never get tired of this view, do we?" Sunny Jim puffed on his cigarette. He was looking at the bay and the islands. "One of these days I'm getting a boat and I'll be out there waving at you and Diane." His hand described that wave and the smoke lifted off his fingers.

It was a dream, Marjorie knew it would never happen for him, but she pictured it as real... Sunny Jim afloat in a big dishtub, smiling, waving, happy as he left a trail of smoke in his wake, on his voyage across the sea.

63
A TIN PEACH CAN

Marjorie was tired when she drove home at night. Her legs were sore, her feet, she could feel the place on her arms where she rested plates. She never expected to be at the Nimbus this long, it was her first job with Labor Now and she stuck with it. She was better at holding on than Voyd. Marjorie wanted to be part of his world, even if that wish pulled her a hundred million miles. But he was having the same trouble on this planet that he had on Mars. Blown like a paraffin flower seed, Voyd was always floating ahead, as if his feet were never on the ground. When could he ever catch his breath? He kept promising his time was coming sooner or later. She didn't think of time that way, for her it was here now.

Forest Street turned into Garden Street, traffic lights and brake lights.

Searchlights on Jupiter Hill played across the

dark sky. Americans didn't have a MarsCorp reward waiting for them and neither did she and Voyd anymore. They only had each other.

That must have been why she stopped at the curbside.

She got out of the little cardboard car. It wasn't disguised as anything it wasn't.

An orange Ford Millipede was parked in front of her. As she went to the sidewalk, she read the bumpersticker CIA-029 K48 and groaned, "I know, I know!" Their new radio convinced them MarsCorp was going to catch everyone in holograms unless they entered the code.

She felt a raindrop on her face. Just one. That's the way it starts. One raindrop sent ahead of a cloud. It might take a few minutes for the rest to let go and fall. They weren't sure. The ground was a long way below. The cloud might decide to go somewhere better.

The man at the table held an open umbrella over his chair, ready for the rain that would make a soft landing and slide to a puddle on the sidewalk. Other places raindrops could land were in the waterglasses and cups cluttered along the tabletop. There was room for rain in each one. Marjorie wasn't looking for rain though, she wanted to look at their tropical fish. The city had a lot of streets to cover and tables like this one appeared then disappeared along with blanket magic carpets spread on the cement loaded with bootleg tapes, electronics, knockoffs and the shiny things that were candy to Earthlings. Voyd and Marjorie were moths to them too. Voyd often bought flowers that turned into weeds. That was the problem with holograms, you never really knew what they were hiding. But Marjorie learned to be careful. There are certain things to notice. She could spot them in the fins and scales where the color fell out of the image like a crayon.

The guy with the umbrella was listening to a Martian radio. He was chewing a toothpick, staring at a spot in the sky imagining the game of baseball. When Marjorie set some of her tip money in the shoebox, he didn't seem to notice.

A scattering of rain drops pearled on the car roof. She carried a tin peach can with an orange goldfish in it. It looked like the genuine article, they were common in the pet stores all over the planet. There are even goldfish beyond Earth. She and Voyd had one when they got married. She picked this fish mostly because it reminded her of those days before Warbler Street, when they were just married and living in a bubble on Mars.

a magic regard for water

64
The SAME FISH

The rain was distracting Marjorie driving home. Part of the problem was she didn't want to use the windshield wipers. Martians are born with a magic regard for water. She couldn't disturb their paths on the glass. She didn't notice if the robot was making progress. Its silhouette would be blended with the billboards and trees. For a moment when she got home, she remembered it and wondered if the robot would be standing in their yard in the rain. The moonlight on the prairie next door. The church bells ringing on the other side of their duplex.

Warbler was calm. No sign of a robot.

Voyd made his famous peaches meal and she cherished a Postum on the couch afterwards.

The goldfish found a place to swim on the bookshelf. She didn't care if the fish wasn't real, for now it was. Part of the fun of a hologram was finding out what it would turn into. But if it was real, it would stay this way, and she was sure it would. The next day, she would find out she was right. After the holograms from Mars vanished without a trace, she fed the same fish in the morning and also at night.

Marjorie and Voyd were soon lying on the couch watching a movie. It didn't take Marjorie long to close her eyes. She was warm. A dream was coming for her, unrolling like the blanket fields of Taraxacum. They vowed to stay awake for the robot, but Marjorie was already asleep under Voyd's arm.

Voyd could feel she was sleeping. He didn't mind, he would wake her when the robot arrived. It could be hours. They were prepared. He turned off their hologram as soon as he got home. There was no point in it anymore. Their duplex looked strange attached to a blue cathedral, but it stayed that way as the sun went down and the carnival shined around them.

The telephone rang. "What?" Voyd reached over the couch to get the phone off the table. "Hello?"

A voice he didn't recognize asked, "Is your hologram running."

"No, it isn't."

The caller tried again, "Is…Is it running?"

"We're having it looked at tomorrow," Voyd promised. When *none* of them will be running, he thought.

Whoever it was ended the call.

Voyd returned the phone to the table, disturbing Marjorie again.

"Who was that?"

"I don't know. Someone wanted to know if our hologram is running."

She opened her eyes and stared at the ceiling.

Voyd sighed, "No more brownstone…"

"Voyd!" she sat up on her elbow, "Don't you know? That's an old Earth joke, it's one of the oldest in the book." She laughed, "It's called a prank call."

"Well, I don't understand the point of it."

"Oh Voyd," she yawned, "get used to it."

"I'm trying. Believe me."

along the telephone poles

65
TAKE YOUR TIME

It took all day and deep into the night for the robot to reach their house. There had to be unintentional casualties along the way, uprooted lampposts, footprints, and a flattened car or two. It could claim it was only following orders, that's what robots do, sorry, pardon me, moving as slowly and carefully as it could, directions chirruping in its head.

The robot didn't ask for this, it had a life of its own, a farmhouse and a family to look after. Built for a sort of Wichita city on Mars, it had a job walking along the telephone poles, untangling lines, making repairs after the windstorms. Being on the road was hard, lonely work. Then it was drafted to Earth to do the same thing. They stored it for later in a warehouse on the waterfront. Now that it was reactivated it had no idea what happened, this wasn't Mars...so it started walking,

223

looking for anything that might help it find its way home.

A big shadow edged along the bare roof of a duplex.

Voyd woke. He sensed it outside the window in the moonlight. "Did you hear something?"

Marjorie mumbled.

Voyd listened for a minute.

The robot scratched on the door downstairs.

It took a step backwards towards the street and halted, shadows from it thrown every which way by the surrounding kaleidoscope holograms. The robot hissed a cloud of steam. A red light was blinking in it, this was its destination. Once this mission was accomplished, it hoped it could leave Earth.

Don't worry, it will. When MarsCorp was undone, when the factory on Jupiter Hill was shut down, padlocked and handed to the forest, the robot would return to that Wichita-like plain with an aqueduct that ran through it like Interstate 135. The rocks bounced around its feet raising dust on its run towards their farm.

Voyd opened the door and there it was. The robot was standing in their yard with laundry lines strung to its legs. One metal arm held up an umbrella skeleton antenna, raised like a television aerial.

The robot watched as the two Martians crossed the ragged lawn and stopped next it.

Holding Marjorie's hand, Voyd floated with her off the ground to the access panel. The hatch sensed them and popped open. Inside the robot was an illuminated keyboard of numbers and letters. If he didn't enter the code, MarsCorp was going to trap everyone in their holograms, fold them up and throw them away. Humanity would disappear. Voyd and Marjorie already talked it through—they were with the underground— there's no reason people and Martians can't live on Earth together.

Voyd said, "Here we go," and he typed in: CIA-029 J48.

"Authorization for this content failed," a mechanical voice buzzed.

"Ooops," Voyd said. "I did it wrong…"

Marjorie gave his hand a gentle squeeze, "Try it again, Voyd…You can do it. Take your time this time."

66
REST

Joan Crawford lived in a dark wood, in a hollow tree. The wolves were restless. They padded in a line along the path they had worn smooth. When they stopped by the fence, they listened to something prickling beyond the dull hum of Aurora Avenue. Whatever it was, it was close. One by one they began to howl. Anyone who lives near the zoo hears that eerie animal cry from time to time. Then it stopped. In that moment Joan Crawford received CIA-029 K48 and responded. She was done, she could rest in wax, in the spring she'd be a queen to the bees. All the holograms were gone. The howling was gone. The pen around her was filled with sheep.

12/12/23

library birdhouses

AFTERWORD

Now that it's over, how did this adventure begin?
My friend Aaron and I were on our way to get
coffee, and we stopped at one of the free library
birdhouses on the Forest Street sidewalk. They're
a little like slot machines put up around town,
but I have had some luck with them. I found the
Thesaurus of Humor that features in *Half a Giraffe*.
Another time I found Suzuki's Zen book. On this
late morning I found *Danny Dunn and the Weather
Machine*. Mainly it appealed to me for the drawings
which are by Ezra Jack Keats. Also, it had a strange
inscription on the inside cover:
CIA-029 K48.

A I
In th

Irene and Joe
the kitchen and ai

"Okay," Dann
Irene."

Rather nervous
bluish rays focuse
pot on the stove.

Suddenly from
burst wild cries.

Danny froze.

Over the soup
Its top was piled
heads; below, it wa

"What—?" Dan

The cloud bo
darker. From it ca
A little bolt of ligl
cloud and struck
Then, suddenly, it
the stove. . . .

We joked about what that might mean. Across the street from the old firehouse, we checked another book box and Aaron found a 1970s book of Texas tall tales. To his surprise, when he opened the book, it also had that strange code! This got my attention. When you're a writer, it's not hard to believe there are invisible forces at work, inspiration is an interplay, and it's appearing everywhere. We soon got our coffee and were talking about 1950s Mexican movies and Aaron told me about a wax museum he went to in Tijuana, mostly to get out of the heat, into their air-conditioning. Suddenly I imagined the AC isn't working and all the stars are melting. And that was the start of this book.

HOLOGRAMS from MARS

Written

end of summer into winter

from *The Trillium Witch* (2021)

Books by Good Deed Rain

Saint Lemonade, Allen Frost, 2014. Two novels illustrated by the author in the manner of the old Big Little Books.

Playground, Allen Frost, 2014. Poems collected from seven years of chapbooks.

Roosevelt, Allen Frost, 2015. A Pacific Northwest novel set in July, 1942, when a boy and a girl search for a missing elephant. Illustrated throughout by Fred Sodt.

5 Novels, Allen Frost, 2015. Novels written over five years, featuring circus giants, clockwork animals, detectives and time travelers.

The Sylvan Moore Show, Allen Frost, 2015. A short story omnibus of 193 stories written over 30 years.

Town in a Cloud, Allen Frost, 2015. A three part book of poetry, written during the Bellingham rainy seasons of fall, winter, and spring.

A Flutter of Birds Passing Through Heaven: A Tribute to Robert Sund, 2016. Edited by Allen Frost and Paul Piper. The story of a legendary Ish River poet & artist.

At the Edge of America, Allen Frost, 2016. Two novels in one book blend time travel in a mythical poetic America.

Lake Erie Submarine, Allen Frost, 2016. A two week vacation in Ohio inspired these poems, illustrated by the author.

and Light, Paul Piper, 2016. Poetry written over three years. Illustrated with watercolors by Penny Piper.

The Book of Ticks, Allen Frost, 2017. A giant collection of 8 mysterious adventures featuring Phil Ticks. Illustrated throughout by Aaron Gunderson.

I Can Only Imagine, Allen Frost, 2017. Five adventures of love and heartbreak dreamed in an imaginary world. Cover & color illustrations by Annabelle Barrett.

The Orphanage of Abandoned Teenagers, Allen Frost, 2017. A fictional guide for teens and their parents. Illustrated by the author.

In the Valley of Mystic Light: An Oral History of the Skagit Valley Arts Scene, 2017. A comprehensive illustrated tribute. Edited by Claire Swedberg & Rita Hupy.

Different Planet, Allen Frost, 2017. Four science fiction adventures: reincarnation, robots, talking animals, outer space and clones. Cover & illustrations by Laura Vasyutynska.

Go with the Flow: A Tribute to Clyde Sanborn, 2018. Edited by Allen Frost. The life and art of a timeless river poet. In beautiful living color!

Homeless Sutra, Allen Frost, 2018. Four stories: Sylvan Moore, a flying monk, a water salesman, and a guardian rabbit.

The Lake Walker, Allen Frost 2018. A little novel set in black and white like one of those old European movies about death and life.

A Hundred Dreams Ago, Allen Frost, 2018. A winter book of poetry and prose. Illustrated by Aaron Gunderson.

Almost Animals, Allen Frost, 2018. A collection of linked stories, thinking about what makes us animals.

The Robotic Age, Allen Frost, 2018. A vaudeville magician and his faithful robot track down ghosts. Illustrated throughout by Aaron Gunderson.

Kennedy, Allen Frost, 2018. This sequel to *Roosevelt* is a coming-of-age fable set during two weeks in 1962 in a mythical Kennedyland. Illustrated throughout by Fred Sodt.

Fable, Allen Frost, 2018. There's something going on in this country and I can best relate it in fable: the parable of the rabbits, a bedtime story, and the diary of our trip to Ohio.

Elbows & Knees: Essays & Plays, Allen Frost, 2018. A thrilling collection of writing about some of my favorite subjects, from B-movies to Brautigan.

The Last Paper Stars, Allen Frost 2019. A trip back in time to the 20 year old mind of Frankenstein, and two other worlds of the future.

Walt Amherst is Awake, Allen Frost, 2019. The dreamlife of an office worker. Illustrated throughout by Aaron Gunderson.

When You Smile You Let in Light, Allen Frost, 2019. An atomic love story written by a 23 year old.

Pinocchio in America, Allen Frost, 2019. After 82 years buried underground, Pinocchio returns to life behind a car repair shop in America.

Taking Her Sides on Immortality, Robert Huff, 2019. The long awaited poetry collection from a local, nationally renowned master of words.

Florida, Allen Frost, 2019. Three days in Florida turned into a book of sunshine inspired stories.

Blue Anthem Wailing, Allen Frost, 2019. My first novel written in college is an apocalyptic, Old Testament race through American shadows while Amelia Earhart flies overhead.

The Welfare Office, Allen Frost, 2019. The animals go in and out of the office, leaving these stories as footprints.

Island Air, Allen Frost, 2019. A detective novel featuring haiku, a lost library book and streetsongs.

Imaginary Someone, Allen Frost, 2020. A fictional memoir featuring 45 years of inspirations and obstacles in the life of a writer.

Violet of the Silent Movies, Allen Frost, 2020. A collection of starry-eyed short story poems, illustrated by the author.

The Tin Can Telephone, Allen Frost, 2020. A childhood memory novel set in 1975 Seattle, illustrated by author like a coloring book.

Heaven Crayon, Allen Frost, 2020. How the author's first book *Ohio Trio* would look if printed as a Big Little Book. Illustrated by the author.

Old Salt, Allen Frost, 2020. Authors of a fake novel get chased by tigers. Illustrations by the author.

A Field of Cabbages, Allen Frost, 2020. The sequel to *The Robotic Age* finds our heroes in a race against time to save Sunny Jim's ghost. Illustrated by Aaron Gunderson.

River Road, Allen Frost, 2020. A paperboy delivers the news to a ghost town. Illustrated by the author.

The Puttering Marvel, Allen Frost, 2021. Eleven short stories with illustrations by the author.

Something Bright, Allen Frost, 2021. 106 short story poems walking with you from winter into spring. Illustrated by the author.

The Trillium Witch, Allen Frost, 2021. A detective novel about witches in the Pacific Northwest rain. Illustrated by the author.

Cosmonaut, Allen Frost, 2021. Yuri Gagarin stars in this novel that follows his rocket landing in an American town. Midnight jazz, folk music, mystery and sorcery. Illustrated by the author.

Thriftstore Madonna, Allen Frost, 2021. 124 summer story poems. Illustrated by the author.

Half a Giraffe, Allen Frost, 2021. A magical novel about a counterfeiter and his unusual, beloved pet. Illustrated by the author.

Lexington Brown & The Pond Projector, Allen Frost, 2022. An underwater invention takes three friends through time. Illustrated by Aaron Gunderson.

The Robert Huck Museum, Allen Frost, 2022. The artist's life story told in photographs, woodcuts, paintings, prints and drawings.

Mrs. Magnusson & Friends, Allen Frost, 2022. A collection of 13 stories featuring mystery and magic and ginkgo leaves.

Magic Island, Allen Frost, 2022. There's a memory machine in this magic novel that takes us to college.

A Red Leaf Boat, Allen Frost, 2022. Inspired by Japan, this book of 142 poems is the result of walking in autumn.

Forest & Field, Allen Frost, 2022. 117 forest and field recordings made during the summer months, ending with a lullaby.

The Wires and Circuits of Earth, Allen Frost, 2022. 11 stories from a train station pulp magazine.

The Air Over Paris, Allen Frost, 2023. This novel reveals the truth about semi-sentient speedbumps from Mars.

Neptunalia, Allen Frost, 2023. A movie-novel for Neptune, featuring mystery in a Counterfeit Reality machine. Illustrated by Aaron Gunderson.

The Worrys, Allen Frost, 2023. A family of weasels look for a better life and get it. Illustrated by Tai Vugia.

American Mantra, Allen Frost, 2023. The future needs poetry to sleep at night. Only one man and one woman can save the world. Illustrated by Robert Huck.

One Drop in the Milky Way, Allen Frost, 2023. A novel about retiring, with a little help from a skeleton and Abraham Lincoln.

Follow Your Friend, Allen Frost, 2023. A collection of animals from sewn, stapled, and printed books spanning 34 years of writing.

Holograms from Mars, Allen Frost, 2024. Married Martians try to make do on Earth in this illustrated novel.

Books by Bottom Dog Press

Ohio Trio, Allen Frost, 2001. Three short novels written in magic fields and small towns of Ohio. Reprinted as *Heaven Crayon* in 2020.

Bowl of Water, Allen Frost, 2004. Poetry. From the glass factory to when you wake up.

Another Life, Allen Frost, 2007. Poetry. From the last Ohio morning to the early bird.

Home Recordings, Allen Frost, 2009. Poetry. Dream machinery, filming Caruso, benign time travel.

The Mermaid Translation, Allen Frost, 2010. A bathysphere novel with Philip Marlowe.

Selected Correspondence of Kenneth Patchen, Edited by Larry Smith and Allen Frost, 2012. Amazing artist letters.

The Wonderful Stupid Man, Allen Frost, 2012. Short stories go from Aristotle's first car to the 500 dollar fool.

Milton Keynes UK
Ingram Content Group UK Ltd.
UKHW020656260224
438492UK00017B/850